THE PLANTATION BOSS

The dream of Kerry's life had been to trace her two lost sisters – and at last she had done it! One, Michelle, was poor and in need of help; the other, Avril, was a wealthy heiress living in Barbados and well able to supply it. The only snag was Wayne Harvey, Avril's uncle and keeper of the purse-strings, who was not convinced that Kerry was anything but a cheap little gold-digger!

R 1678

THE PLANTATION BOSS

BY
ANNE HAMPSON

MILLS & BOON LIMITED
17–19 FOLEY STREET
LONDON W1A 1DR

First published 1972
This edition 1972

© Anne Hampson 1972

ISBN 0 263 71345 8

Made and Printed in Great Britain by
C. Nicholls & Company Ltd
The Philips Park Press, Manchester

CHAPTER I

For the past fifteen minutes Kerry Fairclough had been sitting in the office of Lee, Haslett & Grindley, outlining her life's history before finally coming to the point of her visit.

"I've recently had a thousand pounds left to me and I'm willing to spend the whole sum in finding my two sisters."

Thomas Haslett cleared his throat, leant back in his chair and, eyeing Kerry from under bushy grey brows, explained that his son would be in shortly and would be most interested in her case.

"Anything in the nature of an investigation is right up his street," the old man went on, smiling faintly. "He should have been a detective, not a solicitor."

"You don't consider the task impossible, then?" Kerry's voice was eager, her large hazel eyes bright with hope "It's such a long while, and I haven't the faintest idea where they are." Kerry turned her head as a younger man entered the office. The introductions were made and, having shaken hands with Kerry, Stephen Haslett took possession of the chair opposite to her, examining her face as he did so.

"Miss Fairclough's been talking while we were waiting for you," said his father. "And, briefly, the case is this: thirteen years ago, when Miss Fairclough was ten years old, her parents were killed in a train disaster. Miss Fairclough and her two sisters, one aged three years and the other only one month old, then came into the care of the local authority. But later each child was adopted by a different couple. Miss Fairclough, having recently come into some money, wishes us to discover the whereabouts of her sisters."

A slow frown had been gathering on Stephen Haslett's face as his father spoke.

"They used to do that sort of heartless thing in those days," he remarked angrily. "But now the authorities are much more humane, being reluctant to split up families in this way. However, that doesn't help you," he added, then paused, stroking his chin thoughtfully. "I'm keenly interested in your problem, Miss Fairclough, and shall do my utmost to bring about the reunion you desire." Another pause, and then, in a most brisk and business-like manner, Stephen Haslett went on to warn Kerry that the investigation was by no means a simple under-taking, and she must not become impatient.

"I shan't do that," Kerry assured him, adding, "I haven't seen Avril and Michelle for thirteen years, so I can contain myself a little while longer." Yet despite this as-sertion Kerry's voice contained an element of impatience and, noting it, Stephen Haslett smiled.

"I'm expecting another client," said Thomas Haslett, glancing at his watch. "Are you taking Miss Fairclough into your own room?" Stephen nodded and stood up. "If anyone can find your sisters for you," went on the old man, his eyes twinkling yet sympathetic, "it's Stephen. As I remarked before he came in, he should have been a detective."

A few minutes later Stephen Haslett was questioning Kerry, every word being taken down by his secretary. Stephen wanted to know why Kerry had not made any previous move to discover the whereabouts of her sisters, and Kerry explained that she had never before had the money for the investigations and went on,

"My adoptive parents were comfortably off and I re-ceived a very good education, attending university until a year ago. My parents, however, separated three years ago and both have now remarried. It wasn't convenient for me to live with either of them," she continued a little sadly, "and so I decided to share a flat with a friend. I've been earning my own living for just over a year and I expect I should eventually have saved enough to pay for the investigations. However, a few months ago my aunt died – She was my adoptive mother's sister," Kerry went on to explain in response to the interrogating glance shot at her by Stephen. "She left me this money and that's why I'm now in a position to make inquiries regarding my sisters' whereabouts."

"I see. . . ." The young man became thoughtful. "Have you any idea at all where your sisters might be?"

Kerry shook her head.

"Originally we lived in Cumberland, my real father being a farm worker, and so we were quite poor, living in a tied cottage, I remember."

"How did your parents come to be travelling without their children?" Stephen Haslett wanted to know, and Kerry glanced quickly at him, the question appearing to be irrelevant. However, she replied, in her quiet, pleasantly-modulated voice,

"Mother hadn't been well after the birth of Michelle and the doctor arranged for her to see a specialist in Kendal. Father went with her, and the farmer's wife looked after Avril and Michelle. I was at school, of course."

Stephen Haslett made no comment for a space and then,

"Your younger sister was the first to be adopted, I suppose?"

Kerry nodded.

"Yes. But it wasn't long before Avril was also adopted. She was three and a half years old –" A little catch entered Kerry's voice. "I remember it so well – the feeling of utter

7

loss and emptiness on finding myself alone with the foster-parents in whose care we had all been placed."

Stephen nodded sympathetically. He was nice, she thought, soft and understanding and compassionate.

"You were ten years old; people aren't so keen on adopting children of that age."

"No. But eventually I was adopted and I happened to be fortunate in my parents. They denied me nothing and I shall always be grateful for the education they gave me."

"You don't live with them now, though." Stephen spoke to himself, absently fingering the pen on his desk.

More questions presently followed and then Stephen reminded Kerry again that his task would not prove to be easy.

"The thousand pounds," she quivered. "Will it not be sufficient?"

"It isn't a lot of money these days, Miss Fairclough. Those two girls went to different homes, and naturally there will have to be two separate lines of enquiry. But I assure you we shall be as careful as possible with our expenses." Stephen stood up as he spoke, going on to say he would be in touch with Kerry just as soon as the first clue came along. "You'll be anxious to know how the investigations are progressing." Kerry rose as Stephen opened the door.

"Thank you, Mr. Haslett." She stepped into the musty, brown-linoleumed corridor. "I'm sure you'll do everything you can, and my only anxiety at present is that the money won't be adequate."

He smiled at her.

"We'll trouble our heads about that when the necessity arises – if it does arise. Good afternoon, Miss Fairclough."

Kerry worked in a newspaper office; she had asked for the afternoon off in order to pay this visit to the solicitor, and an hour after leaving Stephen Haslett she had arrived home, to find a dainty tea already prepared by Irene, the friend with whom she shared the flat.

"How did you go on?" Irene looked interestedly at her, one ear alert for the kettle, which she had just plugged in. "Any hope?"

"Yes, they were quite optimistic, though they hinted that it would most probably take time."

"Which you expected, of course."

Kerry nodded.

"All the same, I hope it doesn't take too long, for time means money, and I should hate to have the money run out before Avril and Michelle were found."

Irene hesitated a moment and then,

"Don't bank too much on finding them – well, on finding them both, I mean."

Kerry swallowed hard.

"Something might have happened to one of them?" Irene frowned but said nothing and Kerry went on, "I've thought of that – but they're both very young. Avril's going on seventeen and Michelle's only thirteen. Surely they're both still living."

Irene glanced at her and disappeared into the kitchen. Kerry heard her pouring water into the teapot and then she reappeared, carrying a tray which she set down on the table. Kerry's brow was puckered; she was wondering if she were doomed to some sort of disappointment. Despite her optimism of a moment ago she could not help having doubts. Thirteen years was a long time and things could have happened to one – or even both – of the girls. And if she did find them, would they be as she had always pictured them? – gay and pretty and full of life? She had been so sure they were *nice* girls, that they were responsible people, people with high ideals, but these days there were so many of the others about – so many abandoned people who lived for the day. Fear suddenly welled up within Kerry and for one panic-stricken moment she almost wished she had not set in motion the investigations that could very easily end, for her, in disillusionment and heartache.

"They must be nice, and good," Kerry told herself in a sort of urgent desperation. "They must be!"

Little did Kerry know that the money left by her aunt was to bring her trouble and heartache in plenty ... but in a very different way from anything she could have visualized.

It was almost a month later when Stephen Haslett rang. Irene answered the phone and called excitedly to Kerry, who was in her bedroom, having just come in from work.

Taking the receiver from her friend, Kerry listened eagerly, her eyes aglow with excitement.

"Yes, I'll come along tomorrow. Can you possibly see me during the lunch hour?"

"You're working? Er – yes, I expect I can arrange it. Just one moment." Kerry heard the rustle of pages being turned and then, "Yes, come along tomorrow at half past twelve."

"They've found Michelle!" Kerry was trembling as she replaced the receiver and turned to her friend. "I can't believe I'm really going to see her! Just think, Irene, she was only about three months old when I last saw her – she was adopted very quickly, as I told you." Silence fell on the room and then Irene asked about Avril.

"Mr. Haslett mentioned complications but didn't sound unduly perturbed. I shall know all about it tomorrow – Oh, Irene, I can hardly wait!"

Irene smiled, happy for her friend. Dark and pretty, she was two years older than Kerry, and was to be married very shortly.

"What else did he say?" she asked. "Did he tell you all

about Michelle? Did he say where she was living?"

"No, he – he. . . ." Something prickled in the region of Kerry's spine as her voice trailed away into silence. "He didn't tell me anything at all." Bewilderedly she looked at Irene. "Isn't that odd?"

Irene frowned at her friend's expression.

"Didn't you ask him about Michelle?"

"I did begin to do so." Kerry stopped, thinking hard in an endeavour to remember exactly what was said. "I felt so excited that I just listened. And then when I began to ask about Michelle Mr. Haslett interrupted, suggesting I go to the office tomorrow."

Irene's frown deepened, but she spoke lightly in an effort to assuage Kerry's fears.

"I expect he was too busy to talk on the phone; solicitors usually are. You'll know all about it tomorrow, as you've just said."

"That was Avril I was talking about, not Michelle." Kerry's voice was low; her eager excitement was suddenly like dust in her mouth. "Mr. Haslett could have told me more, Irene, much more. All he said was that they'd had difficulty in tracing Michelle, but at last they'd found her. Then Mr. Haslett spoke about Avril, mentioning the complications –" Kerry's voice took on an even lower note as she added, "Why did he evade my question about Michelle? He did evade it, Irene, I can see that now."

A tiny sigh escaped her friend; she said soothingly,

"I'm sure everything will be all right, Kerry. Mr. Haslett would have said if something were seriously wrong. Don't spend the rest of the evening worrying, for there's nothing you can do until tomorrow."

Promptly at twelve-thirty Kerry presented herself at the office, and immediately she had accepted the chair offered she inquired, rather breathlessly,

"Michelle . . . she's all right?"

"All right?"

Kerry looked at Stephen Haslett. Was it imagination, or did his eyes betray an element of concern?

"You said so little on the phone last evening, and I wondered – wondered if there was anything wrong."

Stephen did not reply immediately, but sat back in his chair, thoughtful and quite obviously turning something over in his mind. At last he gave a sigh of resignation and said,

"I didn't say much on the phone, you're right. I felt it was better to talk here. Miss Fairclough, your young sister has not had a very happy life with her adoptive parents –"

"Not happy!" Kerry stared at him, her heartbeats quickening. Somehow she had always surmised that her sisters had both been as fortunate as she. "Have you seen Michelle, Mr. Haslett?"

He nodded.

"Yes, I've seen her." Stephen Haslett paused a moment. "At the time of the adoption the parents believed they were incapable of having children, and in fact Mr. and Mrs. Johnson did not have a child of their own until Michelle was seven years old." Stephen Haslett looked at Kerry as he added, "They had another child two years later, then came twins. Last year another child arrived, so that makes five little ones . . . and Michelle, who is thirteen." He stopped, inviting some comment, but Kerry did not speak and he continued, "I expect, at the time of the adoption, the necessary inquiries were made about this couple, and I've no doubt that they did at first make good parents. But what I saw of the man I certainly didn't like. He's an invalid and that might have brought about a change in his character –"

"Mr. Haslett," interrupted Kerry, "are you saying that

12

this couple are unkind to Michelle?"

A small pause and then, reluctantly,

"Your sister, Miss Fairclough, is little more than a drudge. The mother has to work, supplementing what the State provides. Her husband can just about mind the little ones while Michelle's at school, but it's she who prepares the midday meal – and also the evening meal, I expect, for the mother doesn't get home from work until after six o'clock. When I called – unexpectedly, of course – Michelle was in the kitchen surrounded by dirty clothes, which she was washing in the sink." Stephen became silent, watching Kerry. Her face was pale, the hand resting on the desk opened and closed automatically, revealing her disturbed emotions.

"This is awful." She spoke in a husky tone, aware of the sympathetic gaze of the young solicitor. "Is there anything I can do? I mean – can I take Michelle from these people?"

Stephen Haslett was shaking his head even before she had finished speaking.

"I did tentatively suggest, when I saw what was going on, that they be relieved of Michelle, but the child is obviously too useful to them. Also, in about three years she'll be working – bringing in money." Stephen shook his head again. "They have everything well considered, Miss Fairclough, and all you can do is wait until your sister is old enough to leave them and come to you – if she should wish to, that is."

"I can go and see her?"

"There was no objection, for like sensible people they've let Michelle grow up knowing she was adopted. However, Mrs. Johnson made a firm stipulation that you must write first, telling her when to expect you."

Write. . . . Kerry's lips curved bitterly. She must make an appointment to see her own sister.

13

"My other sister," she managed at last, deliberately tearing her thoughts away from Michelle. "You mentioned complications."

"Until this morning there did appear to be complications, because Avril lives abroad –"

"Abroad?"

Opening a drawer, Stephen Haslett withdrew a cable and, laying it on the desk, he stared at it thoughtfully for a long while.

"A fortnight ago we received information that Avril was adopted by a couple whose home was in Barbados," he said at last, absently fingering the cable. "At that time they were on a year's visit to England, having come for the sole purpose of adopting a child. Our informant couldn't tell us more than that, so I immediately sent over a young friend of mine who has made extensive enquiries – so he tells me in this cable, which arrived only this morning. Your sister's still living on the island." Stephen's mouth took on an ironical twist as he again perused the cable. "Avril has fared much better than her sister; her father and mother are both dead and Avril is now a wealthy heiress, her assets being enormous."

Kerry stared, and swallowed a hard little lump in her throat. One sister a wealthy heiress and the other just a little slave!

"Avril. . . . She's not yet seventeen. Is someone looking after her?"

"An uncle – her adoptive father's unmarried brother. He manages Avril's vast sugar plantation along with his own." Stephen glanced up and added, "That's all I know at present, for the contents of the cable are naturally brief. I hope to be in a position to give you further information in about a week's time."

She nodded, and as the mention of the cable brought monetary matters to her mind she said,

14

"This trip to Barbados – it must have taken a good slice out of my money?"

"I'm afraid so, Miss Fairclough. But you did express your willingness to spend the whole thousand pounds."

"Yes – oh, I'm not complaining, Mr. Haslett. I was just afraid that the money might be running out."

"It has practically run out, the greater part having gone on the tracing of Avril. I believe there will be about a hundred pounds left." He smiled then and added, "Just about enough to pay your fare out to Barbados to see Avril."

"But not enough to get me home again," she murmured, and Stephen Haslett's brows went up a fraction.

"I expect your sister will see that you have the money for that."

Absently Kerry nodded. Avril would be so thrilled at seeing her sister that she wouldn't mind in the least paying the fare home. A moment later Kerry's thoughts had returned to Michelle as she glanced down at the paper in her hand. Northenhurst . . . a village in Kent.

"I'll write to Michelle's mother this evening," she said, in a flat dejected voice. "Did she give any indication that I might have to wait before I could visit my sister?"

Stephen Haslett shook his head.

"No, she merely stated that she must have warning of your coming."

Kerry stood up.

"Thank you for all your work, Mr. Haslett. You'll be in touch immediately you have more news of Avril?"

"Of course, Miss Fairclough. I'll telephone you at once."

It was a week later that Kerry received a reply to her letter. Michelle's mother wrote in pleasant terms, saying Kerry could visit her sister the following Sunday afternoon. Kerry showed the letter to Irene, who read it carefully.

15

"The woman's fairly well educated," was Irene's first remark on handing it back. "And it's not an unfriendly letter. Perhaps things are not quite so black as your Mr. Haslett painted them."

"I don't know," sighed Kerry, folding the letter and returning it to its envelope. "I soon shall, though," she added, suddenly wondering how she would feel at the moment of reunion. Inevitably there must be an awkwardness, she thought. But that would soon disappear and then she and Michelle would have each other, for always. "My original intention is not going to materialize," she said, speaking her thoughts aloud. It was Wednesday morning; she and Irene were just preparing to sit down to breakfast, and Kerry went into the kitchen to fetch the coffee pot.

"The grand reunion of the three of you, you mean?" Irene was at the sideboard, taking cutlery from the drawer. "No, I don't expect that can come about for some years – unless your wealthy sister coughs up the money for Michelle to have a holiday out there on that marvellous island."

"I expect she'd do that willingly," returned Kerry, but added, "Whether or not Michelle's parents would let her go is another matter."

"In the meantime, you'll be going out to Barbados alone?"

"I think so, yes." Kerry had returned to the dining-room and she looked at Irene, a shade of uncertainty in her eyes. "If Michelle's people are so poor, I suppose I should let them have the hundred pounds."

Irene frowned at this idea.

"Not at all. You've spent all your legacy on finding your sisters, just for the joy of a reunion, and I don't see why you should be denied this joy. A hundred isn't much to spend on yourself in any case. No, I'm definitely not

16

in favour of your giving that last hundred away."

Kerry sat down at the table, but made no attempt to eat as she pondered over her friend's words. No, she would not part with her last hundred for anything except her fare to Barbados. She must see both girls.

"I'll have to write to Avril first," she said after a while. "Won't she be surprised?" A smile came then and Irene smiled and nodded in response.

"Surprised and happy. I think it's wonderful – what you've done with your aunt's money, that is. Do your parents know about these investigations?"

"I wrote to them both, explaining what I intended doing." Kerry stopped and gave a tiny sigh. "I haven't had a reply from either of them."

"Too busy with their own concerns." Irene's mouth compressed a little. "These days people are so wrapped up in their own affairs that they seem to have lost both the ability and the desire to trouble their heads about anyone else."

"I wonder what Avril's like?" Kerry spoke speculatively, ignoring her friend's remarks. "I expect she's very sophisticated and confident, having been brought up amid so much wealth."

"She's a lucky little blighter, and it's to be hoped she appreciates her good fortune." Irene poured Kerry's coffee and then filled her own cup. "This uncle – I suppose that, in effect, he's her guardian?"

Kerry nodded, helping herself to toast and butter.

"I expect he is."

"Do you know his name?"

"Only his surname. Avril's father's name was Harvey, so his brother's will be the same."

On the Saturday afternoon Kerry went shopping, buying presents for Michelle and her mother, and sweets for the younger children. But all the while she was in a state

of ever-increasing uneasiness and concern about her forthcoming visit to Michelle and her parents. If Michelle were
not being treated properly how could she, Kerry, stand
aloof, voicing no complaint – ? Determinedly Kerry
checked her thoughts. As Irene had said, things might
not be so black as Mr. Haslett had painted them.

The small council house was jammed almost suffocatingly
in between its squalid neighbours. The front "lawn" put
Kerry in mind of a mangy cat she had once seen, while
the small surrounding border supported nothing more
colourful than a few struggling dandelions and a patchy
carpet of dull-green moss.

Standing on the front doorstep for a few seconds Kerry
heard the cry of a child from somewhere at the back of
the house, then some sharp unintelligible words from a
masculine throat. She knocked, startlingly aware that her
nerves were fluttering and her legs felt like jelly.

The door was opened by a woman of about forty years
of age; she looked pinched and tired but was neatly dressed – for the occasion, mentally concluded Kerry on noting the touches of powder and lipstick and the newly-
washed but rather frizzy hair. Obviously the woman
could not afford to visit a hairdresser.

"Miss Fairclough?" The woman was as awkward as
Kerry felt. "Do come in – Michelle's just gone to the corner shop for some bread. We run short, you know, with
there being so many of us." Mrs. Johnson stepped aside
and Kerry entered the narrow passage off which led the
fairly large sitting-room and the kitchen. "In here. . . ."

Kerry stood in the doorway a moment, staring at the
man on the couch. Very soon she was surrounded by
children – the twins, aged three, a little girl of about four,
and a boy – obviously the eldest of the Johnson children
– of about six years of age. From the back garden came the

cry Kerry had previously heard and as her eyes strayed to the window she saw the pram. The man rose lumberingly from the couch and extended a hand.

"Pleased to meet you, Miss Fairclough. Won't you sit down?"

"Thank you." The children followed her into the room, then stood there, staring at her. She noted their clothes – clean but poor. Her eyes wandered round the room and she shuddered. On embarking on this idea of finding her sisters she had not thought to discover such a contrast in the circumstances of the two. It had always seemed natural to picture each in a situation similar to her own, and it had come as a shock to discover that one sister was possessed of great wealth while the other lived in poverty.

"Off you go and play!" The sharp voice of their father instantly had its effect upon the children, who disappeared through the door leading into the kitchen. From her hard-seated upright chair Kerry saw them troop into the garden. Her parcel was down on the floor beside her chair; Mrs. Johnson was asking if she would care for a cup of tea.

"I would – thank you very much."

"This is a great surprise to us, Miss Fairclough," the woman's husband remarked when he and Kerry were alone. "We knew of course that there were three of you, but once a child is adopted it tends to become completely cut off from the rest of its family – or so it was in those days." He stared at Kerry, examining her with faint interest. His eyes moved from her lovely face to her hair, shining like pure bronze laced with strands of gold. Her wide brow was puckered, her mouth quivering slightly. She controlled it, managing a smile. "You're not a bit like Michelle," was the man's comment at last, and Kerry gave a little start. She remembered that Michelle had her own colouring, as did Avril, and with the passing of the years Kerry had visualized both girls as resembling herself, at least to some degree. "Michelle's very fair – platinum blonde, with blue eyes."

Kerry looked at him; how odd that this man should be telling her what her own thirteen-year-old sister looked like! Kerry's eyes turned to the garden.

"She's – she's here now. . . ." The girl, slender to the point of unnatural thinness, had entered the garden by the back gate and was now coming towards the house, a wrapped loaf under her arm, her eyes on the window, expectant, yet timid and a little uncertain. Kerry's mouth felt dry as she heard the woman say, from the kitchen.

"Your sister's come, Michelle. Go and say hello to her."

Michelle stood shyly in the doorway; Kerry rose and took one step forward, then stopped, the dryness in her throat preventing speech. This was the supreme moment for which she had longed – to come face to face with one of her sisters. It was the reward for which she had considered her legacy well spent, and now she could only stand there, for how long she would never know. But she did know that Michelle's eyes were misted, her young lips quivering, while Kerry, herself deeply moved, found her thoughts too profound for utterance and, oddly, it was the younger girl who eventually broke the spell, coming forward slowly into the drab room, holding out a hand and stammering awkwardly,

"How d-do you do? I'm pleased to m-meet you." Michelle's hand was rough with work, but her clasp was warm and firm. Kerry's fascinated stare was still fixed on her sister's face. What a beautiful child! So nymph-like and ethereal, such tender delicate lines to her face – and the eyes! Deepest blue, soft and pensive and undeniably sad.

"Michelle. . . ." The word broke at last and then the sisters were embracing, forgetful of the man on the couch or the woman who had come to the kitchen door in order to witness the meeting. "How wonderful to see you –" Kerry kissed the child, then held her away, laughing and crying as she added in cracked and husky tones, "You don't remember me at all, but I remember you. You were so small and cuddly...." Kerry's voice trailed away into an emotional silence. Michelle spoke again, both her hands now clasped in those of Kerry.

"Mother and Father said I had two sisters and I've often tried to imagine you both." She shook her head and as she did so two great tears escaped to roll down her cheeks. "You're not a bit as I imagined you to be. I mean," she added hastily, "you're much nicer."

"Nicer?" Kerry glanced swiftly at the woman in the doorway. She would have loved to be alone with Michelle for a while, but there was nowhere they could go – unless it was to a bedroom. "How do you mean?"

"Well ... with your being ten years older I expected you to be rather stodgy and – sort of – superior. But you look so young – much younger than twenty-three. And you're pretty...." Michelle gazed at Kerry, gazed her fill and sighed deeply. "I'm so glad you decided to find me. Father told me how you were left some money by your aunt." Michelle's voice was soft and finely-toned, her smile tremulous and very sweet.

"So am I glad I decided to find you," returned Kerry, still in husky tones. "You're very beautiful, Michelle."

A small laugh then, and Michelle wiped away her tears.

"You're not disappointed in me. Oh, you have no idea how afraid I've been!"

"She's a silly one," put in Mrs. Johnson, though not unkindly. "We kept on trying to reassure her, but the way she's worried since Mr. Haslett came is just nobody's business."

"I was afraid Kerry would take one look at me, decide

I wasn't what she had expected, and go away, and I'd never see her again."

"I'm sure your sister would never be so unkind as that," said Mrs. Johnson, turning back into the kitchen as the kettle began to whistle on the stove.

"No, she wouldn't, I see that now," was Michelle's confident rejoinder. "I'll never be afraid again."

The two girls continued to stand there, hands clasped, while Kerry explained that Avril also had been found, but suddenly Kerry turned as if drawn, and the expression she saw on the man's face set all her nerves tingling. Stephen Haslett had emphatically declared that he did not like this man, and Kerry had no doubts about the young solicitor's shrewdness and ability to assess a person's character.

"Very touching," said the man, little or no expression in his tone. "Very touching indeed."

Michelle blushed and withdrew her hands.

"I'll help Mother with the tea," she murmured, and Kerry caught her lip between her teeth as the child disappeared into the kitchen. The man had interrupted a scene which Kerry had fervently wished to prolong; his very presence now jarred. She looked at him; found him faintly revolting in his premature obesity, and in the fact that he required a shave. He was an invalid, she suddenly remembered, but could not revise her opinion of him. Kerry sat down again, her eyes on the kitchen door, for she was eager to catch every move of the lovely child who was flitting about, now setting crockery upon a tray, now placing spoons in the saucers, now opening a packet of biscuits. At last the tray was brought in by Mrs. Johnson and placed on the table. Michelle was still in the kitchen and as she listened Kerry heard the conversation between her and one of the children.

"Michelle, I've cut my finger on some glass – ooh, it

does hurt! Are you going to bandage it up for me?"

"Yes – let me see. It'll have to be washed first. Hold it under the tap. . . ."

A short while later, as Kerry drank her tea, another child came into the kitchen. Michelle was just telling the first child to be more careful in future, and added,

"Keep the plaster on, because if you don't you'll get dirt in your cut and it will turn septic."

"Michelle, I want a sandwich!"

"I want a drink of water." This voice was small and Kerry guessed it belonged to one of the twins.

"Ask Tommy to get you some water. I'm making Bridget a sandwich. And besides, I want to go in to my sister."

Frowning darkly, Kerry looked at the woman sitting at the table, her teacup to her lips.

"Isn't Michelle coming in to have a cup of tea?" she couldn't help asking, her tones crisp, to say the least.

"Yes – er – of course. Michelle!" the woman called. "Come and have your tea."

"She's seeing to the children's needs." Mr. Johnson spoke abruptly and almost challengingly, his eyes on Kerry. "Michelle has to do these jobs, Miss Fairclough. She's old enough and sufficiently capable, and neither my wife nor I believe in spoiling children." He stared hard, fairly inviting some protest which, Kerry did not doubt, would be dealt with instantly it was uttered. Kerry remained silent, her thoughts involuntarily straying to Avril – Avril who had everything.

Michelle came into the room at last and, sitting down at the table, poured herself a cup of tea.

"I'll have mine filled up." Her father held out his cup; rising, Michelle took it from him, filled it and walked over to the couch with it, glancing at Kerry as she passed her, and smiling winsomely so that Kerry's heart-strings were suddenly caught and jerked.

"May I take Michelle out to tea?" asked Kerry a short while later. "I saw a very nice restaurant on the main road as I came along on the bus. I expect they open on Sundays?"

"They do open, yes, but as I've said, Michelle has her jobs to do."

Michelle was clearing away the teacups, piling them on to the tray, but she stopped what she was doing and said pleadingly,

"Can't I go, just this once? Please, let me, Father."

"And leave your mother to look to all the children? Certainly not." He glanced at Kerry. "Sorry to disappoint you, Miss Fairclough, but Michelle is needed here." Firm the voice and although Kerry's blood boiled she managed cautiously to curb the retort rising swiftly to her lips.

Michelle was almost in tears; her lips quivered and she seemed deliberately to be avoiding her sister's anxious gaze.

Unable to leave without making some endeavour to get Michelle away, Kerry asked if she could speak to Michelle's parents alone.

"It's something important?" Without waiting for an answer Mr. Johnson inclined his head in the direction of the door and Michelle immediately went out.

Kerry scarcely knew how to begin. For one thing, Stephen Haslett had already made the request which was now in Kerry's mind, and for another, there was no certainty that Michelle would wish to leave her parents. The child was used to the position of near servility, had grown up with it and as such it was a habit by this time – a habit which she might have no inclination whatsoever to break. Perhaps, thought Kerry in her sudden indecision, this was not the time. Perhaps she should wait until Michelle knew her better. If she could have Michelle at the flat for a while.

"You have something to say to us, Miss Fairclough?"

Mr. Johnson spoke at last and Kerry was forced to reply.

"I wondered if – if you'd allow Michelle to have a holiday with me?"

The man's face twisted in a clear assumption of pained asperity. Kerry felt her temper flow like fire through her veins.

"Haven't I just said Michelle is needed here? Holiday? Why should she have a holiday when we ourselves haven't had one for seven years?"

"As we have only just found one another," said Kerry, amazed at her patience and restraint, "I feel it would be nice for us both to have – well, a week together."

"Don't you work?"

"I do, but I could get a week off."

"No need. Michelle stays here."

Kerry turned to the woman. She was just a timid automaton as far as Kerry could see and her expression took on a hint of contempt. Nevertheless, she said, forcing a smile,

"Mrs. Johnson, wouldn't you like Michelle to have a holiday with me?"

"Well . . . you see, Miss Fairclough, I've to work – I did explain this to your solicitor. And so Michelle has to see to the kiddies – my husband being ill."

Ill . . .? Kerry glanced at him, searching his face.

"Is it something serious, Mr. Johnson?"

"The old heart. Can't do heavy work, and as my job's in building that's me finished for the rest of my life."

"Not if we get that business you're always talking about," put in his wife, a sigh in her voice, yet a forced optimism also.

"How are we to get the money for a business?" he snapped impatiently.

"Well . . . you go on the pools, and you're always saying we'll have a business of our own yet."

"You could manage a business?" Kerry asked the question impulsively, the germ of an idea establishing itself in her mind.

"The corner shop's coming up for sale in three months' time. I could manage the office side; Mother could do the counter work."

Kerry pursed her lips, her idea growing steadily.

"How much are they asking for this business?" she inquired, and both the man and his wife looked at her in swift surprise.

"Three thousand pounds."

Three thousand pounds. . . . And Avril a wealthy heiress. Surely there would be no difficulty in persuading Avril to pay this sum. The uncle, though. In all probability he had control of her money. Still, he would understand – yes, Kerry was convinced he would readily allow Avril to provide the money which would free Michelle. Although aware that her idea was well ahead of the present situation Kerry said,

"If I could get the money for that business, would you let me take Michelle to live with me – let me have her unconditionally?"

A rather stunned silence followed before the woman spoke.

"We would never part with Michelle –"

"Keep quiet," interrupted her husband curtly. "Miss Fairclough, are you serious about this offer?"

Looking at him and noting the avaricious expression in his eyes, Kerry experienced the greatest difficulty in hiding her contempt.

"It wasn't an offer, Mr. Johnson, because I myself don't have that sum. But I might be able to obtain it." She stopped, looking at Mrs. Johnson. The woman's mouth was trembling and it was clear that she did have some sort of affection for Michelle. This knowledge could not influence Kerry, though, for she was thinking only of her sister's welfare – her happiness and her future – and she asked again about having the child to live with her.

"If you can give me the three thousand – yes, you can take Michelle."

"Then I'll do my best, Mr. Johnson." Kerry glanced towards the kitchen door. "Can I see Michelle for a moment or two?"

"Of course you can." The man called to Michelle, who was washing the dishes. His wife was sitting there, her head bent, and Kerry bit her lip, wondering if the woman were crying. Kerry looked from her to the slender girl standing in the doorway, drying her hands on a towel. Her sweet young face was pale, her eyes tired and dull. Kerry swallowed something hard and painful in her throat.

"Goodbye for the present, Michelle dear." Taking the child in her arms, Kerry kissed her; Michelle clung almost desperately when at length Kerry tried to move away. Both Michelle's parents were watching the scene, but the two sisters were totally oblivious of them. "I'll come again soon." Automatically Kerry turned to the man. "You won't mind if I visit Michelle regularly?"

"Come whenever you like." The man was eager; he added significantly, "We might be doing business, Miss Fairclough?"

"Yes, Mr. Johnson, we might." Only after she had left did Kerry remember that she'd left her parcel down by the chair.

A thunderstorm was just breaking as Kerry came from the house and ran for the bus shelter. The sky was darkened by an enormous cumulo-nimbus cloud; everything was blanketed in dismal grey, with nothing to relieve the gloom.

"Suits my mood at the moment," Kerry said as she

stood there, waiting for a bus which would inevitably be late. Unhappily she recalled her excitement and optimism when on receiving the legacy she made the decision to spend it on finding her sisters. All she had gained up to now was this deep anxiety which had replaced her natural buoyancy. But it was a temporary state, she told herself, for it was only a matter of time before, with the three thousand in the bank ready to hand over, she would be given the custody of Michelle.

On reaching the flat Kerry again found her tea ready and over the meal she related most of what had happened during her visit to Michelle. But she refrained from voicing her intention of trying to get the three thousand pounds from Avril, mainly because the matter was so much in the air at present. Time enough to tell Irene when Kerry had been to Barbados and seen her sister.

"The poor kid's had a raw deal, that's for sure," commented Irene when at last Kerry had ended her narrative. "Let's hope everything's as it appears where Avril's concerned. It would only need something to be wrong there for me heartily to wish you'd never come into that money."

Kerry said nothing. Whatever the outcome of her visit to Barbados, she did at least know Michelle's whereabouts, and even should the plan she had in mind fail, Kerry could live with the knowledge that some day Michelle would be free to leave the Johnsons and come to live at the flat with her.

Later in the week Kerry heard from Stephen Haslett and the following day she went along to the office in her lunch hour. Stephen first asked about Kerry's visit to Michelle, and as with Irene, Kerry omitted any mention of her idea.

"It's tragic that Avril should have a surfeit of this world's goods while Michelle has nothing – but there you are, that's the way it goes." He sighed, fingering his blotter absently. "However, let's get down to the contents of this letter I've received from Mick – he's the friend who's done the investigating for me in Barbados. He's staying on another three weeks, incidentally. Having only his hotel bill to find he decided to take a holiday, and should you decide to go to Barbados immediately you could meet him."

"I'd like to do that," was Kerry's eager response, and Stephen Haslett promised to make the arrangements as soon as Kerry had decided on the date of her departure. Stephen went on to say he now had Avril's address and so Kerry could write to her at once.

"She lives with her uncle, Wayne Harvey, at his magnificent plantation house, even though she has an equally magnificent house of her own." Stephen handed Kerry the paper on which was written Wayne Harvey's address in Barbados – Trade Winds Estate, St. Mark. ... "You certainly need have no anxiety over Avril," continued Stephen Haslett when at length Kerry brought her attention from the paper in her hand. "This uncle of hers guards both her money and her person – she happens to be quite extraordinarily pretty," added Stephen with a faint smile. "This physical attraction plus the fact of her being a wealthy heiress naturally attracts many undesirables and fortune-hunters of all kinds, but according to Mick it's just hard luck for anyone who thinks they can part Avril from her money, be the hopeful male or female. Apparently Avril's uncle is up to every single trick."

"Trick?" Kerry frowned uncomprehendingly.

"You know how it is with a wealthy young girl. Clever rogues concoct all sorts of schemes for transferring a little of that wealth to themselves. But Wayne Harvey appears to be quite competent in dealing with them."

"I'm glad he is," returned Kerry fervently. "It's reassuring to know that he looks after Avril so well – and it's obvious that he thinks a great deal about her." Kerry paused, then added, "Is he her legal guardian?"

Stephen nodded.

"Yes; he's also the sole trustee of her money until she reaches the age of twenty-five." Stephen was absently perusing the airmail letter again, but after a while he said, "This guardian of Avril's is, according to Mick, more than ordinarily formidable, actually being feared on both plantations – but highly respected, nevertheless, as his kind usually are."

Kerry absorbed that, but in a rather abstracted sort of way, for her thoughts were on Avril, picturing her surrounded by luxury, living a life of ease and pleasure on that coral island in the sun, dining at plush restaurants, wearing expensive clothes and having native servants to wait on her, and while she naturally felt glad that Avril had been so fortunate, Kerry was, paradoxically, straining at the unfairness of fate in providing so lavishly for one sister while doling out to the other the meagre necessities of life.

"It'll all be put right, though," Kerry assured herself as she left the office. "Wayne Harvey will be only too willing to let Avril provide the three thousand pounds."

On the day of her departure Kerry received a letter from Mrs. Johnson, and as she read through it the colour gradually drained from her face.

"Something wrong?" Irene stared at Kerry in concern. "Not bad news at a time like this, I hope."

Unable to speak Kerry handed the letter to her friend.

"Dear Miss Fairclough,

I feel I must write to you, for I am greatly troubled. Last Sunday my husband was cross with Michelle and in his anger he said it would be a good thing when she went to live with her sister. I had no intention myself of saying

30

anything to Michelle until this matter was settled, because you had not definitely promised to get the money for us. Michelle was naturally very surprised that there had been any talk of her going to live with you, and because of her affection for me she firmly declared she would not do so. However, she often says how much she likes you, and I know that she is happier now than she has been for some time, happy in the knowledge that she has someone of her own flesh and blood.

As the day wore on I noticed a look on her face I have never seen before and somehow I knew that she was visualizing just what a change it would make to her should she go to live with you. Often she must have compared her lot with that of other girls of her age. She has no life of her own, never has pleasure or wears pretty things. Our house being small she does not even have the privacy of a bedroom of her own, being forced to share with the twins. When, later, she had the opportunity of speaking to me alone she asked about this question of her living with you and I had to tell her what had transpired between us on the day my husband spoke about the business. Despite her feelings for me I could see Michelle was ready to consider leaving us. I too, think it will be a good thing and I told her so. Perhaps I should not have done this because I soon noticed an excitement about Michelle, knew that she was coming to accept the idea of living with you. Should she be disappointed it will break her heart – and mine, incidentally, for I love Michelle enough to want her to be happy. Please, Miss Fairclough, try to find that money, both for Michelle's sake and for mine.

Please do not mention this letter to my husband when next you visit us.

Yours sincerely,
Ada Johnson."

A heavy frown had been gathering on Irene's face as she read the letter and now, still holding the several sheets of paper in her hand, she looked interrogatingly at Kerry. Before she could voice her question Kerry began to explain, adding,

"I haven't mentioned my idea to anyone, not even the solicitor, because there was no certainty of my getting the money." Kerry stopped, her face still white, and a little drawn. "Irene . . . supposing Avril doesn't produce that money?"

Irene gave a sigh and shook her head.

"It would have been better had you seen Avril before making the suggestion – but I expect you see that now."

"Indeed I do," was the fervent reply, and then, "I'm sure Avril will be only too willing to help, though. You think so, too, don't you? I mean – wouldn't you help your sister if you were as rich as Avril?"

"I would, yes, and so would most other people. But –" Irene stopped, unwilling to add to Kerry's anxiety. "Let's look on the bright side," she went on at length. "No use worrying unnecessarily." She glanced at the clock. "You'd better go and finish your packing; the taxi will be here in ten minutes' time."

Kerry nodded, dismissing the possibility of a disappointment for Michelle. Avril would readily produce the money, not only to relieve Michelle's suffering, but also because it would mean a reunion between all three sisters.

CHAPTER II

DURING the flight Kerry had for the most part been uneasily picturing the meeting between Avril and herself. That her sister lived on the island of Barbados was

32

certain . . . and yet Kerry had not received a reply to either of her letters. On sending off the first one, which merely contained a brief explanation and the promise by Kerry of an early visit, Kerry had immediately contacted a travel agent, decided on a date for her flight, then asked her boss to bring forward her holidays from July to May.

Not unduly perturbed by the non-receipt of an answer to her letter, Kerry sent another, presuming that in the first instance something had gone wrong in the post. When the second letter went unacknowledged Kerry naturally experienced some misgivings, but with her flight booked, and her boss having accommodatingly arranged for a stand-in at the office, Kerry decided to go ahead with her plans. It was just possible that both her letters had gone astray – or both Avril's replies – she kept telling herself.

The plane was due to land on the island at seven o'clock in the evening – too late for a visit to her sister, and Kerry had asked Stephen Haslett to request his friend Mick to book her a room at a hotel. Stephen had readily done this; he had also arranged for Mick to meet Kerry at the air-port and to her relief the young man was there, complete with hired car, and Kerry being on her own, Mick soon picked her out and introduced himself.

"It's very kind of you to go to all this trouble," she said as Mick put her suitcases into the back seat of the car. "It makes life so much easier when one has help of this kind."

"I'm only too glad to do it." Mick glanced oddly at her as, opening the door, he waited for her to enter the car. "Stephen wrote saying you hadn't had replies to your letters."

"No, I haven't," admitted Kerry on an anxious note. "And now that I'm here I feel almost apprehensive of calling on Avril." She turned her head as Mick slid into the driver's seat and prepared to start the car. "It would be awful if she didn't want to see me." The idea had never occurred to Kerry until, seeing the islands strung like exotic jewels floating on the dazzling Caribbean, the full impact of what she had done hit her with force. She was here – the island of Barbados was one of those down there – and very soon she would be knocking on a strange door, asking to see Miss Avril Harvey . . . and Kerry was in ignorance of whether Avril would be glad to see her or not.

"She'll want to see you," declared Mick, pressing the starter. "Your sister's not only a stunner beauty-wise, she's also a very charming girl."

"She is?" Stephen Haslett hadn't said anything about Avril's character – probably because Mick had not seen the necessity of mentioning anything about it. "You've met her?"

"At a party one evening," Mick nodded. "I managed to get myself invited so that I could pump your sister –" He broke off and a grin spread over his round good-looking face. "The watch-dog of an uncle didn't leave us alone for long, though. But in a way I wasn't sorry he'd joined us; it gave me an opportunity of weighing him up." Mick had the car on the main highway now and as it sped smoothly along Kerry's attention was caught by the flowers, which at this time of the year were in their full glory, the gardens of the elegant villas being ablaze with exotic colour – pink and white of oleander, the orange and crimson brilliance of bougainvillea, the large showy flowers of hibiscus ranging from creamy white to pink and the more brilliant and spectacular scarlet. Giant palms and other tropical trees waved gently against an azure sky as the north-east trade winds blew in from the sea.

"What is Wayne Harvey like?" Kerry asked, her mind

34

still partly on the beauty through which they were passing.

"Well. . . ." Slow the word and oddly illuminating even in itself. "In his mid-thirties, I should say at a rough guess. Very tall and lean; extraordinarily handsome in that severe, he-man sort of way women go for –" Mick stopped, darting Kerry a swift glance that revealed the humorous twinkle in his eyes. "At the party it was quite clear that there were as many young hopefuls interested in Wayne as there were in his niece – of a different sex, of course," he ended with a laugh.

"If he's so attractive it's a wonder he's not married by now."

"The confirmed bachelor type; self-sufficient and faintly scornful of women – No, that's not strong enough by any means. He appeared immeasurably bored by their chatter and frivolity."

"Yet he attended the party."

"That puzzled me as the evening wore on, but then I decided he had come only for Avril's sake; obviously he wouldn't allow her to attend such an affair unescorted."

"You had some conversation with him?" They were purring smoothly along a palm-shaded drive now, already in the hotel grounds, and Kerry caught sight of a fabulous swimming-pool, and beyond that, a sunken garden and tennis courts.

"A little." Mick paused, frowning but faintly amused, judging by his tone of voice. "I'm quite sure he had his suspicions about me – I felt he regarded me in the light of a fortune-hunter who had chosen Avril as his prey. It'll be a clever man who succeeds in winning your sister for a bride."

"She'll be her own boss some day, though," Kerry suddenly retorted, faintly surprised to discover she was a little piqued by the fact of this unknown Wayne Harvey's having control both over Avril's money and her actions

– which was a ridiculous attitude really because Kerry was inordinately thankful that her sister had the protection of a man who was obviously more than a match for any would-be shark.

"Yes, she'll be her own boss some day." Mick spoke musingly as he brought the car to a standstill at the entrance of the Crescent Moon Hotel. "Nevertheless, I feel that her uncle will still exert a good deal of influence over her, for she certainly likes and respects him."

"He was quite nice with her, then?" Strangely Kerry had pictured Wayne Harvey as a strict, and not very patient, guardian. And yet she should not have come to a conclusion like that because Wayne had taken Avril to the party which, from what Mick had said, was not exactly his idea of entertainment.

"Very nice indeed with her, yet I had the impression that he could be stern, and that Avril accepted his word as law." Mick drew up and a porter appeared immediately to carry Kerry's luggage up to her room. "Shall I take you out to dinner?" Mick obviously wanted to do so and Kerry smilingly accepted the invitation. "Good, then I'll collect you in about an hour. Will that give you long enough to titivate up?" he ended, grinning.

"Just about – and thanks a lot for asking me."

"A pleasure. I shall thoroughly enjoy my last evening on the island."

"Of course – you're going home tomorrow. Mr. Haslett did tell me, but I'd forgotten."

"Sad I am – but determined to return when funds allow – or when some charming young lady wants me to do some investigating for her," he added twinklingly. "'Bye for now; I'll take you to the Miramar – elegant and dignified – a little formal, but the food ...!" They had been standing by the car and Mick slid into his seat. Kerry smiled and waved, then followed the porter up to a mod-

36

est but comfortable room on the fourth floor. It looked out over the gardens to the turquoise sea beyond. There was a bathroom and soon Kerry was taking a shower, her thoughts straying to Wayne Harvey, and she found herself trying to form a mental picture of him from what she had been given.

Tall and lean and handsome; the he-man type women go for – yet he himself was disdainful of women, bored with their feminine trivia. A watchful guardian, yet kind to his ward; a competent and shrewd businessman, obviously, for he managed two vast sugar plantations on which an army of labourers was employed.

Mick was waiting in the lounge when Kerry came down about an hour later; on the way to the Miramar he made a detour so that he could show her where Avril and her uncle lived. Kerry gasped at the splendour as, having stopped the car, Mick indicated the palatial mansion set in enormous grounds. They got out of the car and stood looking through the high wrought-iron gate. Exotic trees of every variety adorned the gardens; an illuminated fountain of crystal clear water provided a fairy-tale-like quality to a scene which was already one of dazzling enchantment.

"He has his own private beach," Mick informed Kerry. "And I believe the inside of the house is absolutely magnificent. But many of the houses on this island are. You have ex-film stars living here, and ship-owners, and of course the wealthy sugar planters. Many of the houses were built in the eighteenth and nineteenth centuries when splendour and elegance were the order of the day. The wealth on these islands just has to be seen to be believed."

Kerry was speechless, merely gazing in wonderment at the mansion but thinking about Avril – and Michelle.

"My sister has a house like this, you say?" she murmured at last, and Mick nodded.

"Not too far away. Both estates join because of course they were owned by brothers."

"It's fantastic!"

"Dazzled by it, are you?"

"Quite dazzled." Tomorrow she must enter these grounds, introduce herself to the girl who lived in all this luxury. . . .

Mick drove to the Miramar, where they dined and danced. But they left early, Kerry being tired, and Mick having to return the hired car, as his flight was at four in the morning.

Mick was unlocking the car door when two couples passed, going towards the hotel entrance, and so he was not aware of the arrested attention of one of the men, nor of the swift yet penetrating stare to which seconds later he subjected Kerry. She herself noticed, but attached no importance to it and, therefore, made no mention of the incident to Mick, to whom she was saying goodbye a short while later when he dropped her at the Crescent Moon Hotel.

"Good luck with the forthcoming meeting," he said, preparing to drive away. "I hope things turn out as you want them to."

But although she smiled and said she was sure they would, Kerry suddenly felt an unaccountable loss of spirit.

A few minutes after paying the taxi-driver Kerry was walking along an avenue of graceful palms. Reaching the impressive front door of Wayne Harvey's house, she stood a moment, surprised and half-ashamed to find herself trembling. Shaking off this absurd nervousness, she reached for the knocker. A dusky maid immaculate in starched white opened the door.

"I'd like to see Miss Avril Harvey," smiled Kerry.

"Your name, please?" The girl looked hard at her; Kerry had the odd impression that she was expecting her.

"Miss Kerry Fairclough."

The girl nodded and bade Kerry enter.

The elegant drawing-room into which Kerry was shown literally took her breath away.

"Please wait," said the girl, and disappeared. Kerry stood by the window, looking around with wide-eyed admiration. Contributing to the impression of harmony and good taste were several handsome pieces of Chippendale and Sheraton furniture, fine wall tapestries of exquisite colour and design, superb Spode and Wedgwood china. Floor-to-ceiling glass doors opened out on to a stone verandah overlooking the landscaped tropical gardens. Beyond this colourful ensemble lay the sapphire bay, part of which was Wayne Harvey's private beach and yacht anchorage.

Suddenly tingling, Kerry turned from her contemplation of the scene outside. Framed in the massive doorway, and evincing no surprise at seeing her again, was the man who last evening had stared so hard and penetratingly at her. How long had he been standing there? she wondered, quite disconcerted both by his silence and by his searching regard. That this was Wayne Harvey she had no doubt, because he was almost exactly as she had pictured him. Almost but not quite, for Kerry now discerned ruthlessness and arrogance in his face. There was a quality of arrogance also in his manner, in the way he looked at her, and even in the way he stood there, one lean brown hand resting on the jamb of the door, the other thrust carelessly into his pocket.

Omitting the courtesy of offering her a chair, he spoke at last, and his voice was so patently inaffable that a chill of apprehension suddenly assailed Kerry and she half wished she had not come to the house, but had tried in some other way to contact her sister.

"I was expecting you, Miss Fairclough. I'm sure you know my name, so I won't trouble to introduce myself. What can I do for you?"

Wayne Harvey had been expecting her, so Avril had obviously received her letters. Why, then, had she not replied? Kerry's thoughts switched automatically to the maid and she knew instinctively that the girl had been warned of her coming – and told what she must do. Kerry looked at Wayne, whose piercing gaze was still fixed upon her. She swallowed, bewildered and dismayed by her reception. Nevertheless, she felt a display of friendliness on her part was essential and, forcing a smile, she extended a hand and said,

"I'm pleased to make your acquaintance, Mr. Harvey. As you know, I came to see Avril." Kerry stopped, disconcerted by the impassivity of the man and by his obvious disinterest. What had gone wrong? she wondered, adding rather lamely, "She's my sister," at which, to her added puzzlement, Wayne's dark brows lifted a fraction. He advanced slowly into the room, an impressive figure in cream linen slacks and an expensively-cut shirt of palest green. His bronzed face was angular and lean, with austere, finely-chiselled features. His hair, dark and straight, was brushed back from a lined and aristocratic forehead, his eyes were the steely-grey of flint – and equally hard. Pointedly ignoring the proffered hand, he watched it fall to Kerry's side, saw her blush hotly at his snub.

"So Miss Harvey is your sister, is she?" Knife-edged, the tone, and distinctly contemptuous. "You have proof of this relationship?"

"Proof?" Kerry shook her head. "No ... I wrote to Avril explaining about the investigations I'd made. She obviously received my letters."

"Your first letter was accidentally opened by my secrerary," Wayne told her smoothly, "and I read it. Your second letter went the way of the first. It was destroyed."

Kerry stared at him in disbelief.

"You kept Avril's letters from her!" she gasped, sudden anger in her voice.

Wayne surveyed her dispassionately, unaffected by her words.

"Miss Fairclough, what benefit did you and your accomplice expect to derive from this little ruse?"

"Accomplice?" she echoed blankly, and a swift intake of Wayne's breath portrayed his exasperation.

"Your friend – the man Mick something or other who came on ahead to discover all he could about my niece, and to pave the way, as it were."

A long silence followed these words as perception began at last to seep into Kerry's brain. Why had not such an eventuality occurred to her? she wondered as snatches of expressions used by Stephen Haslett came rushing back to her: fortune-hunters ... hopefuls, male or female ... clever rogues who concoct all sorts of schemes for transferring some of that wealth to themselves. Avril's uncle was up to every single trick, Stephen had asserted.

"I'm not quite sure what you're accusing me of," she said at last. "But whatever your suspicions I really am Avril's sister. The man you saw me with was no accomplice, as you term it, but the person employed by my solicitor to discover the whereabouts of my sister." She looked up at him, anger rising at his total lack of interest in what she was saying. "I explained in my letters that I had come into some money and had used it on finding my two sisters. One lives in England. . . ." Kerry's voice trailed away into a sort of frustrated silence. Proof could eventually be produced, she knew, but she was here for one week only. "I *must* see Avril," she insisted, her voice rising. "I've come all the way from England for that sole purpose and I'm certainly not returning without meeting her."

Kerry's words fell on deaf ears apparently, for all Wayne Harvey said was,

"I believed I'd heard and seen everything, but this is an entirely new one on me. I repeat, what are you expecting to gain?" He watched her closely, and because the three thousand pounds which would free Michelle had leapt to her mind Kerry blushed, at which his hard eyes narrowed, perceptively, and with acute disdain.

"You're not one of the clever ones, apparently," he observed with a sneer. "Nevertheless, I must hand it to you, the idea was original, and interesting as a consequence, because, as I've said, I believed I'd seen everything." He surveyed her dispassionately, at the same time reaching up to pull the bell rope. "I have never wasted time on you rogues, and this is no exception." He strode to the door. "My servant –"

"But, Mr. Harvey," she interrupted urgently. "My – my fare to England – I haven't any mon –" Too late she tried to check the unthinking utterance and the colour flooded her cheeks as Wayne Harvey swung round, his eyes raking her contemptuously from head to foot.

"My servant will show you out!"

"Mr. Harvey. . . ." Kerry was talking to herself. She heard Wayne's voice outside the door and then the maid appeared.

"I haf to show you out, missy."

Kerry caught her lower lip between her teeth, trying to stem the tears that were already blurring her vision.

"Miss Avril," she began. "Is she in?"

"If you will come this way, missy," said the maid in an expressionless voice, her black hands clasped against her spotless apron.

"What is your name?"

"Cecilia, missy."

"Cecilia . . . would you give Miss Avril a message from me?" This was basically wrong, but Kerry felt that all was fair in the war Wayne Harvey was determined to wage. "I'll give you a telephone number, and please tell her to ring me –"

"I haf to show you out, missy."

Kerry sagged helplessly. And then all the fire that was normally well under control flared. Not often was Kerry in a temper, but when she was she saw red. Brushing past the astonished girl, she ran through the door, turning in the direction taken by Wayne Harvey a few moments ago.

"Mr. Harvey!" she called, injecting an imperious note into her voice. "Come back here; I'm determined to talk to you!" She ran on, wondering through which door he had disappeared.

"Mr. Harvey!" she shouted, her face flushed with anger. "*Mr. Harvey!*"

"What –?" The lovely young girl emerging from one of the rooms glanced in some considerable astonishment at Kerry, before her eyes wandered to the rather frightened face of Cecilia, whose hands were upraised as she muttered something in her own tongue. "Who are you?"

A swift glance round by Kerry, and then in a hushed voice,

"Are you Avril?"

"Yes, but –"

"I'm your sister – I wrote to you, but your uncle kept the letters from you –"

"My sister?" The girl stared for a moment in dumbfounded amazement. "What are you talking about?" she managed at last. "You must be crazy! I have no sister."

Had Kerry's mind not been totally occupied with get-

43

ting in every word she could in case Wayne should reappear she would have stopped to think; as it was she continued urgently,

"Certainly you have – two, in fact. We were all adopted by different parents when our own were killed, you must know this –"

"Miss Fairclough!" Wayne's furious voice cut Kerry short as he came striding through the hall. "Cecilia," he thundered, "I told you to show this woman out! Why haven't I been obeyed?"

This woman! Kerry's fury threatened to choke her and she had to swallow hard before she could speak.

"Your servant did try to show me out, but I was determined to see my sister –"

"Avril is not your sister."

"Uncle Wayne," quivered Avril, white to the lips, "what is this all about?"

"The woman's an impostor –"

"I am not! I . . . ." Kerry's voice trailed away into an appalled silence as, looking from Avril's white set face to that of her uncle, Kerry realized what she had done.

Avril hadn't known she was adopted.

"My – my parents – they *were* my real parents!" The bewildered, pathetic protest was like a knife in Kerry's heart, but even as she began to stammer an apology her arm was taken in a savage grip and she was propelled roughly and with speed the whole length of the hall.

"Cecilia – open the door!"

The girl ran to do her master's bidding and Kerry underwent the supreme indignity of her life. She was quite literally thrown out of Wayne Harvey's house.

CHAPTER III

KERRY sat on her bed, head in hands, wondering if a legacy had ever caused such misery as hers. Although two hours had elapsed since her unceremonious ejection from Wayne Harvey's house she was still trembling and the pulses in her temples throbbed with excruciating pain. Over and over again she lapsed into the gloom of self-condemnation – yet how could she have known what dire results her action would have? With all the good intentions in the world she had chosen what she believed to be the most profitable way of spending the money inherited from her aunt. She had been very close to Aunt Freda, she recalled, and wondered what the old lady would think could she know that her money had been expended merely in buying unhappiness for three people. Bitter tears rolled down Kerry's face as she thought first of Michelle and then of Avril. What was Avril doing now? Being comforted by her uncle, perhaps, and yet Kerry was dismally convinced that no one could comfort Avril at this time. She had loved her parents, who obviously had kept her adoption a secret. Although Wayne Harvey knew, naturally.

"I should have thought of that," she whispered, drying her tears only to encourage the flow of more. "But Wayne Harvey should have told me that Avril didn't know. If only he'd believed me we could have talked, in a friendly way, and I'd willingly have followed his advice." This would have meant disappointment for Michelle, of course, but although the idea of that was painful to Kerry, at least only one of her sisters would have been hurt.

Kerry's unhappy musings were suddenly interrupted by the telephone. A gentleman was downstairs and wished to see her.

"Thank you. I'll be down immediately." Wayne Harvey – it must be, she decided, wondering how he had found her. Her feelings were mixed. Was he here to heap recriminations on her head? – or to ask her to go to Avril? The latter, surely, she thought, her heart lightening a little. Kerry could not see Wayne Harvey coming here for any other reason.

What a sight she looked! Tear-stained face and a bruised arm where Wayne's fingers had so savagely gripped her. Her legs were cut and scratched all over, for when Wayne had given her that final thrust, instead of landing on the path she had found herself staggering through some vicious thorns. Stockings would cover her legs and a cardigan her arm, but there was nothing she could do about her face and with a shrug of resignation she went out and along to the lift.

"Mick!" Disappointment flooded over her even while, paradoxically, she was glad to see a familiar face. "What happened?"

He had missed his plane, having overslept. Being at a loose end because there was not another until the following night he had come along to the Crescent Moon, although he had not really expected to find her in. He stared at her as he explained, taking in the unmistakable evidence of her disappointment.

"Perhaps it's I who should ask you what happened?" he said, and to her utter dismay Kerry started to cry. With male practicality Mick took her arm and steered her gently towards the door leading out into the more private atmosphere of the hotel grounds. Finding a seat in a secluded spot, he pushed her on to it, sitting down beside her. "Better tell Uncle Mick all about it." He gave her a

46

large handkerchief. "Take this – it's creased a bit, but clean."

"Th-thank you." Kerry looked at him. "Mick, it was awful – you've no idea how badly I feel. Everything's wrong." Disjointedly the story came out, the whole of it, and after the small silence following the end of her narrative Mick said oddly,

"It was your intention to get three thousand out of Avril?"

"Don't say it like that, Mick. I didn't think Avril would miss it."

"Mere drop in the ocean," he agreed, but added, "Did you let Wayne Harvey know you were after money?"

"I think he guessed," she had to admit, but hurriedly went on to say she had not been intending to ask for money immediately. "At that particular time my chief desire was a reunion with Avril. I'd been so looking forward to it and – and even now I can't believe I'll never see her again." She bit her lip, trying desperately to stem the tears. "I realize now that I should have written to Wayne first, and not to Avril. I think perhaps he would have looked at the matter in a totally different light if I had."

Ignoring that, Mick frowned heavily,

"That secretary of his, Rowena Blakely, is a bitchy type. She should have given your letter to Avril, not Wayne."

"That's what I thought. Had I opened a letter by mistake I'd certainly have seen it went to the person it was meant for." Kerry paused, dry-eyed now. "What makes you say she's a bitchy type?"

"Perhaps she isn't," he admitted. "But it so happens that I don't like her. She was at the party – playing up to Wayne all the time like some fawning schoolgirl with a crush. Wayne must have been blind not to see it, but as I said, he always appears so utterly bored with women that

47

such behaviour probably goes right over his head."

"I've no quarrel with Wayne now for keeping back my letters," said Kerry, reasonably, dismissing the matter of Wayne's secretary and bringing the subject back on its original course. "He obviously didn't want Avril to know she was adopted. The only thing I blame him for is that he didn't write back to me immediately, explaining the position." She frowned in puzzlement. "As he was so anxious to shield Avril from the truth you'd think he would have made sure I never came to the island at all, and only by writing to me could he be absolutely sure I'd understand, and of course, give up the idea of the reunion with Avril."

Mick sent her a quick glance.

"You're forgetting something, aren't you?"

"Forgetting something?"

"*You* know your motives were honourable, and that you genuinely *are* Avril's sister, but Wayne Harvey doesn't. As far as he's concerned you're an impostor, another rogue – but with a new idea, that of masquerading as Avril's sister –"

"If I weren't genuine I wouldn't know Avril had a sister," cut in Kerry impatiently. "Wayne Harvey should instantly have realized that."

"I'm beginning to think that although Wayne Harvey knew Avril was adopted he didn't know she was one of three sisters. He could have been told she was an only child."

Kerry's eyes opened wide. Wayne Harvey's action, not only in keeping back the letters, but also in failing to contact her, had become more and more puzzling to Kerry. But now she could see reason in his behaviour.

"You mean, that he felt I had somehow come into possession of certain facts about Avril, and that I meant to exploit my knowledge?"

"It's pretty obvious that this was his conclusion."

"It would explain everything."

Silence fell between them for a while before Mick inquired if Kerry had had any lunch.

"No – I couldn't eat – not the way I felt."

"Can you eat now?"

"I think so." Food would be far from appetizing even now, she felt sure, but perhaps it would help to remove the empty, sickening feeling in the pit of her stomach. "Isn't it too late, though?" she added, noticing the seats in the garden filling up, evidence that lunch was over in the hotel restaurant.

"Too late here, but we'll find an eatery somewhere. Are you ready?" It was not with deliberate intention that he happened to look at her as he said this, but Kerry flushed and murmured apologetically,

"I can't do anything about my face."

"I think your face is just about right the way it is." And then, realizing flattery was out of place at this time, "We'll be ten minutes or so in the taxi, so I expect the evidence of your tears will have disappeared by then."

Mick took her to the Carib Inn, three miles north of Bridgetown, and right on the water. A buffet lunch was served despite the lateness of the afternoon. After a waiter had led them to a table on the balcony they ate in silence for a little while and then, with some reluctance, Kerry mentioned her financial position, saying she could not at present obtain money from either of her parents.

"Mother's married to a man who's dreadfully mean," she went on to explain. "And in addition he doesn't like me. So there's no chance of borrowing money there. Father would let me have some – but he and his wife are away in America at present, on a two-month tour of the country. I don't know that I have ever in my life acted so foolishly as I did in coming here," she added. "I had only my single fare."

49

"You – ? He stared, his fork poised half-way to his mouth. "You haven't the money to get home?" he gasped disbelievingly.

Kerry shook her head.

"Looking back, I can't think what made me act in so thoughtless a way. You see, the picture I'd built up was of Avril's being delighted to see me – a grand reunion, as it were. Then we would talk and I'd tell her about Michelle. Avril would then be willing to discuss the transfer of the three thousand to Mr. Johnson in exchange for Michelle's freedom. I'd spent my thousand, so I fully expected Avril either to give or lend me the money for my return fare. I'd also visualized myself living in her house – or, I should say, her uncle's house – during my stay, and I never even thought about such things as hotel expenses. I even saw Avril paying towards Michelle's fare to come over here next year – when I could bring her for a holiday." Kerry shook her head and tears filmed her eyes again. "Never did I imagine a disaster such as has happened. I – I thought my money would bring happiness to all three of us, and instead it's brought nothing but misery."

Mick's good-natured face clouded a moment and then became pensive. He was deep in thought and Kerry did not disturb him. Despite the fact of her mind being occupied with her desperate situation she could not help but be appreciative of the beauty of this coral island in the sun, for it was a veritable realm of sun-drenched enchantment, with colour everywhere – the dazzling, almost unbelievable flame of the flamboyant trees, the delicate violet of the jacarandas and the perfumed beauty of the pink and white oleander blossoms. Tamarind trees and fan palms gave shade to the verandah on which she and Mick were sitting; over the grounds of the restaurant were scattered calabash trees and breadfruits, mangoes and the yellowed-flowered Pride of Barbados. Dotted about the silver beach were almond trees and palms, with here and there a lovely manchineel. All this colour, plus the incredible blue of a West Indian sky and the brittle gold of the sun shining on to the wide spread of the Caribbean where the warm trade winds stirred the surface into white-tipped, aquamarine wavelets rolling lazily on to the shore.

A paradise, thought Kerry, watching the bathers down below, their bodies tawny as an Arab's. How she had looked forward to coming, anticipating a wonderful holiday taken with her sister – bathing, perhaps, and exploring, but talking all the time, for there were thirteen lost years between them. Well, all her anticipated pleasure was as nightshade in her mouth. And for a long, long while to come she must live with this bitterness, engulfed by blame, even while she was totally innocent.

"I've thought of something," pronounced her companion at last, bringing Kerry from her musings.

"Thought of something?"

"We've got to get you out of this predicament – and it seems like fate that I missed that plane." Kerry threw him a grateful look, but he did not appear to notice. "I'd be only too willing to make you a loan, but I'm almost out of money myself, it being the end of my holiday. I reckon you need well over a hundred pounds?"

"My fare, yes, and money for the hotel." She looked fearfully at him. "Mick . . . I have a dreadful feeling that I'm shortly to suffer the ignominy of deportation –"

"Rubbish!" In spite of her expression Mick had to laugh. "Haven't I just said I've thought of something? Now," he continued briskly without waiting for an answer, "you can't get money from either of your parents. Is there anyone else who would lend it to you?"

"No. My friend would have done so in the ordinary way, but she's getting married next month and she's practically spent up – this I know because she's been buy-

51

ing things for their house for weeks."

"Then you must get a job."

"Job? Here?"

"I met a hotel owner during my investigations and became rather friendly with him. He's wanting an English receptionist immediately – male or female – the one he had having left him to get married."

"But, Mick, I don't want a permanent job."

"He has no one at all at present. He'll be only too glad to take you on; it would give him time to find someone permanent. Eat up," Mick added briskly. "We'll go along and see him now."

Kerry was taken on immediately, her speech and appearance instantly having a favourable effect on Mr. Mason, the proprietor of the Beach Manor Hotel, who said that if she changed her mind and wished to stay on permanently he would be delighted.

"Well," said Mick with a satisfied air as they left the hotel where Kerry was to begin work the following morning, "that's eased things up a bit."

Kerry nodded, the merest glimmer of her innate cheerfulness and optimism already penetrating the gloom.

"You know," said Mick reflectively as, later, they sat in the lounge of her hotel, "I don't think you ought to give up so easily as this."

"About Avril, you mean?"

"Yes. Oh, it's true that at this present time she must be feeling very sad, and angry with you, perhaps –"

"Perhaps?" cut in Kerry bitterly. "There's no perhaps about it. Avril must be hating me for what I've done to her." And so would Wayne be hating her, thought Kerry, although his opinion wasn't in the least important.

"True," agreed Mick, leaning one elbow on the table and combing his fingers through his hair in a habit Kerry had previously noticed. "Nevertheless, Avril will eventu-

ally get used to the idea – she'll have to, of course. What I mean is that, having accepted that the parents she knew were not her own, she's quite likely to want you."

"Someone of her own flesh and blood," mused Kerry, borrowing Mrs. Johnson's phrase. "Mick ... do you really think so?"

"It would be the most natural result – at least to my way of thinking." He looked at Kerry and added slowly, "Your job at home – will it be kept open for you?"

Automatically she shook her head, falling once again into a state of unhappy brooding before she replied listlessly,

"I can't see it being kept open indefinitely."

"Nor can I," promptly agreed Mick. "Your job gone, your friend getting married. ... Are you keeping on the flat when she leaves?"

"Of course."

"I expect the rent's quite high? – could be very expensive for one person?"

"It is – yes." Kerry looked swiftly at him, aware now of where these questions were leading, and at the same time remembering her hope that Michelle would come to live with her at the flat.

"I don't know what sort of a salary you were getting in England, but the money here seems extraordinarily good to me." The merest hesitation and then, "Why not stay for a while?"

"Stay?" she repeated, even though the idea had come to Kerry seconds ago as Mick was asking his questions, and in fact she was already well ahead of him, seeing herself able to send money to Mrs. Johnson, so that she could get help in the house to relieve the burden on Michelle. Kerry could also see that Michelle had decent clothes to wear, and pocket money to spend on herself. But Kerry's decision was not so simple, for on the other

side of the scale was the hurt Michelle would suffer on being deprived of the regular visits Kerry had promised to make to her. After moments of indecision Kerry at last chose the way which she believed would be best for the child, and that was for her, Kerry, to remain on the island and send what money she could to Michelle and her mother.

At least one thing had gone right, decided Kerry after having worked at the Beach Manor Hotel for almost a fortnight. Charles Mason was a kind and considerate employer and, seeming to understand Kerry's financial position, he paid her weekly instead of monthly. Some of her first week's money was sent to Mrs. Johnson, and some to Michelle, together with a long letter containing a full account of what had happened. Kerry also expressed deep regret that she could not see Michelle for some time but promised to save and come to England the following year for her holiday. Kerry received an airmail letter towards the end of the following week. It was from Michelle, thanking her profusely for the money and eagerly telling Kerry what she had already bought with part of it.

"Mother says to tell you she is very grateful for what you sent to her and she will write to you very soon. Already she has made arrangements for a lady to come in three days a week and do most of the housework and the washing. I am happy, but sad too, for I was only just getting to know you. I shall write every week, though, and I know you will do the same. Please tell me soon when you will be able to come and see me – so that I can count the weeks and cross them off on my calendar. It is so nice having someone to write to.
                    Your loving and grateful sister,
                            Michelle"

There followed a row of kisses – but no mention had been made of the business. Michelle had hidden her disappointment very well, but Kerry knew that disappointment must have gone very deep.

"If only I'd kept my idea to myself until I'd seen Avril," whispered Kerry unhappily. However, she shook off her dejection, and a deep emotion suffused her whole body as she held the letter in her hand . . . her first letter from a real relation. . . .

Kerry read it three times, then folded it up and put it in the handbag, feeling at this moment that she would carry it about for the rest of her life.

"At least I've made some small reparation for the damage I've done," she whispered as, glancing at the clock, she realized that in five minutes' time she must be on duty. Quickly crossing to the dressing-table she picked up the comb and had just begun tidying her hair when there was a knock on her bedroom door.

"Come in."

Fred, one of the porters, entered, a letter in his hand.

"Sorry, Miss Fairclough, but I brought up only one of your letters. I've just noticed this other one." He held it out and Kerry frowned as she took it from him.

"Thank you, Fred."

He went out and she stared at the envelope in her hand. It had been posted in Bridgetown. . . . Almost feverishly she opened it, her heart leaping as she noted the signature at the bottom of the page.

"Dear Kerry," she read. "Yesterday I lunched with a girl friend at the Beach Manor Hotel. You weren't at the reception desk when we went in, but you were when we came out. You were busy and didn't see me, but I realized you were working there and I feel I must see you. I shall be in the Barbados Museum at three o'clock on Wednesday, which I know is your day off because I phoned the night porter last evening. . . ."

Avril . . . and acting without her uncle's knowledge. But although troubled by this Kerry had no intention of letting slip this opportunity of seeing her sister.

Kerry took a taxi to Garrison, a mile and a half out of Barbados, where the museum was situated. Avril was standing by a case containing old Indian relics, but she turned as Kerry approached and for a moment both girls stood staring at one another, neither able to speak. Avril's face was pale and Kerry thought she was thinner than when she had last seen her, so briefly, only a fortnight ago.

"Avril –" Kerry spoke the one word at last, then spread her hands. "I'm so terribly sorry for what happened. . . ." Her voice trailed away; never had she been at such a loss for words.

"You really are my sister, aren't you?" Avril glanced around as she spoke and it was obvious that she was uneasy, seeming to be half afraid of what she had done in inviting Kerry to meet her.

"Yes, Avril, I am," returned Kerry simply, and then added, "I deeply regret disillusioning you about your parents. I'd no idea you didn't know. . . ." Again her voice trailed away; Avril said awkwardly,

"Is there anywhere we can go?"

"You're well-known on the island, I suppose?" Kerry didn't mean her tones to be stiff, but she knew they were, and forced herself to smile.

"Yes – and I mustn't be seen with you," said Avril desperately. "I can't think of anywhere we can go to talk privately."

"Can we ride around in a taxi?" suggested Kerry, and to her relief Avril's eyes brightened.

"Yes, that's a good idea – oh, and I've just thought of an out-of-the-way little café near Bath, that's on the Atlantic side of the island," she added in case Kerry didn't know. "We'll take the taxi out to it."

As the drive began they talked politely and with a certain tenseness between them, but to the surprise of both the initial awkwardness was soon dispelled; they were eager to learn all they could about each other and a great deal had been said by the time they reached the café, where Kerry dismissed the taxi after making sure she could get another when it was required.

The first thing Avril wanted to know was why Kerry was still in Barbados, and Kerry was guarded without actually telling an untruth.

"I like it here," she said. "And when the job at the hotel was offered me I decided to stay on for a while."

"I'm so glad you did," responded Avril eagerly, and then at Kerry's invitation went on to tell of her life with her parents and, later, with her mother. She mentioned the house and plantation she owned and talked of her life with Wayne, which was undoubtedly happy. For her part Kerry talked of her own life and of her job and the flat she had shared with Irene. And she naturally talked about Michelle.

On entering the café Kerry ordered tea and cakes, which were brought to them at the secluded table they had chosen in the far corner of the restaurant.

"To think ... I have two sisters –" Avril shook her head in an incredulous sort of way and added shyly, "Michelle is thirteen – how old are you?"

"Twenty-three. I was ten at the time of the accident."

Avril's eyes clouded.

"It must have been awful for you. I know because of the way I felt when my mother died – my – my adoptive mother," she corrected slowly and painfully. "I loved her very much." She turned her fair head and looked at Kerry. "I think I hated you at first," she owned with a hint

57

of apology in her voice. "I felt quite ill at that moment and – and when I asked Uncle Wayne if it were true that I was adopted, and he said yes, I just wanted to die."

Kerry bit her lip, and instinctively covered her sister's hand, which was lying on the table.

"I was so utterly stupid. You see, Michelle's parents had told her the truth, as most parents of adopted children do, and I just didn't stop to consider whether or not you were also in possession of the truth. I'm terribly sorry," she ended, a catch in her voice. But Avril was shaking her head.

"I'm not sorry – not now. I think you're a lovely sister to have, and I'm also dying to meet Michelle. But that isn't possible," she immediately added, "not with Uncle Wayne in the mood he's in now."

"No, Avril, that won't be possible – at least, not for some considerable time." Kerry had not previously enlarged on the great difference in circumstances of the two sisters and even now she was guarded, seeing no point in upsetting Avril, who in any case could not help. Wayne Harvey had full control of her money and he would never sanction a gift of three thousand pounds. Besides, as things were he must be kept in total ignorance of any meetings which Kerry and Avril might arrange. They would have to be extremely careful, thought Kerry, not without a tremor of apprehension, for once Wayne Harvey knew she had not left the island he would be instantly on the alert.

"Tell me about my – our real parents." Avril spoke with obvious reluctance and yet with a tinge of eagerness also, and Kerry spoke for several minutes, watching Avril's changing expression as she talked of happy times spent in the country, in the farm cottage in Cumberland in which they had all lived.

"It must have been awful for you," murmured Avril

again, her eyes dark with sympathy. "I don't remember anything, and of course neither would Michelle – but you. . . ."

"It was awful," agreed Kerry in a low voice. "And it was awful losing both my sisters –" She broke off, but her recollection brought a smile to her lips. "I used to love playing house – with you and Michelle as my two children. Michelle was such a dear little baby, and you – well, you've grown up just exactly as I thought you would." Avril blushed with pleasure at the compliment but said nothing and Kerry continued reminiscently, "As I grew older I often wondered where you both were, and I was determined to find you one day and bring about a reunion." Sadly she shook her head. "I went about it the wrong way, I see that now it's too late. I should have written to your uncle, not to you."

"If you had done so I think perhaps he would have agreed to see you and talk. I did ask him to invite you to the house – after several days had gone by and I had not only accepted the fact of my parentage but also decided that you really were my sister. But Uncle Wayne wouldn't even listen – he was so furious with you – and still is," ended Avril regretfully.

"He doesn't know I'm still on the island, obviously."

"No – because I heard his secretary asking about you – she'd heard all about that scene from Cecilia – and Uncle Wayne said he expected you'd left, and he was sure you'd never set foot in Barbados again." Avril flushed on imparting this information and added by way of an excuse for her uncle's conduct, "He was only trying to protect me, Kerry. I do hope you understand?"

Kerry nodded and smiled, reassuring her sister, even though she felt she would never forgive Wayne Harvey for subjecting her to such humiliation.

"He still doesn't believe I'm your sister, then?"

"I don't know about that. For several days after you'd gone he was sort of quiet – and brooding, and I did wonder if he were thinking about you and wondering if you were genuine after all. That was when I suggested he invite you to the house but, as I said, he was so angry that I let the matter drop."

"And then decided to contact me without his knowledge. I'm so glad you did, Avril, even though I'm fully aware that, in a way, it was wrong."

For a moment Avril looked pained, and somewhat guilty.

"I just had to see you, Kerry. And having done so I have no regrets at all. I'm happy to know that I've two sisters and, after a little while, perhaps I can talk to my uncle and bring him round."

"You think that's possible?"

A smile spread over Avril's lovely features.

"He's awfully nice, Kerry – although just now you must be thinking he's very far from nice."

And far from gentle, Kerry could have added wryly, but of course she refrained.

"You're very lucky to have him," was all she said, and Avril nodded in agreement.

"I know I am – and I know I can make him see reason, but I dare not try yet, not while he's so angry with you."

Kerry was silent. If as Avril had just suggested, Wayne was coming to accept the fact that Kerry was not an impostor after all, then his anger now stemmed from the fact of Kerry's having upset his niece by blurting out the truth, and although this did bring a brighter aspect to the situation, Kerry had the dismal conviction that Wayne Harvey would not easily forgive her for the pain and disillusionment she had so unwittingly caused his niece.

On leaving the café – by separate taxis, at Kerry's suggestion – they arranged to meet there the following Wednesday, which they did. And on Kerry's arrival back at the Beach Manor Hotel Charles Mason invited her to dine out with him at Sam Lord's Castle, which was the show place of the whole island, being a one-time plantation house of a Regency buccaneer – the same Sam who hung lanterns to lure ships to their destruction on a reef.

Kerry did not hesitate to accept the invitation, for she liked Charles and even in the short time she had been working for him a friendship had begun to develop.

It would be nice to dress up, she thought, taking out an enchanting green lace cocktail dress from her wardrobe. Her hair had been washed only that morning and it shone, her eyes were bright with a happy expression, for she and Avril were really getting to know one another and the afternoon had been one of the most pleasant Kerry had ever spent.

"You look charming." Charles looked her over as he made his flattering comment. "You blush quite attractively, too," he added with a hint of humour as his eyes at last came to rest on her face.

Kerry laughed; Charles put a hand under her elbow as he led her out to the waiting car.

On the way something went wrong with it and as Charles was poking about under the bonnet for a few minutes the first thing he did after he and Kerry were shown to their table was to go and wash his hands. On his return he informed Kerry that some of his friends were at another table and that he and Kerry had been invited to join them.

"They asked me?" She looked up in surprise, for apart from Charles and Avril, Kerry did not know anyone on the island.

"I was invited to join them and I said I'd a friend with me." Already he was beckoning the waiter, who was told about the change of table being made.

As they walked the length of the restaurant on their way to the other table Kerry saw many eyes turn in her direction. It was one of those occasions when she felt good – her lovely curves provocatively enhanced by the cut of the dress, her hair a glowing mass of bronze sprinkled with gold. Her cheeks were enchantingly flushed, her expression happy because of her recent meeting with Avril. People were walking about, being shown to their places by the waiters, and Kerry was within a few yards of the table when she saw Wayne and his companions – a girl – Rowena Blakely, Charles told her later – a man with greying hair, and a middle-aged woman in immaculate attire who made up the foursome. Kerry's senses tingled and she glanced around with a sort of desperation as if seeking some means of escape. But of course there was no escape. Her employer headed straight towards Wayne's table, as Kerry instinctively knew he would.

Absorbed in conversation with his companions, Wayne was smiling; Kerry noted his sudden upward glance as she and Charles neared his table, saw the smile wiped from his face and watched him make a swift recovery as both he and the grey-haired man rose to their feet. A tense moment existed between Kerry and Wayne as they stood there, Wayne's hard eyes looking out from a set and arrogant face, Kerry palpably unnerved by this sudden encounter, and also hot and embarrassed because of the indignity to which Wayne Harvey had previously subjected her.

No one seemed to notice her discomfiture – it was a miracle, she thought, striving to collect herself, for whatever Wayne's emotions might be at the knowledge that she was still in Barbados, he was to all outward appearances totally unaffected by her arrival on the scene.

Forced by the presence of others to disguise his animosity, he voiced a frigid greeting as he extended a hand, which Kerry took, raising her eyes to his and wondering if he too were remembering his snub on that other occasion.

Where was Avril? Kerry wondered, at the same time immeasurably thankful that she wasn't here to add further tension to what must surely become an overloaded atmosphere.

CHAPTER IV

It went without saying that the dinner to which she had looked forward was completely spoiled for Kerry. Firstly she was acutely aware of Wayne Harvey's deep dislike, and in addition she seemed to be an object of continual interest to his secretary, who was not only ill-mannered enough to stare at Kerry for long moments at a time, but was also rudely condescending in the way she spoke to her, for on hearing Kerry's name Rowena naturally realized who she was.

"Are you staying long on the island, Miss Fairclough?" the girl enquired smoothly when for a while the others at the table were deep in conversation about a new sugar refinery which was being built in Barbados.

"I have no idea how long I shall stay, Miss Blakely." At the stiff politeness in her tone Rowena's dark eyes glinted and Kerry had the strange conviction that she had made an enemy.

Kerry examined the girl's face with some curiosity. Beautiful, she readily owned, while at the same time deciding that the beauty went no deeper than the surface.

The girl had a flawless complexion and very dark eyes; her hair, seductively falling over her cheeks and neck, was also very dark. Yes, Rowena possessed outstanding beauty, but she also possessed a measure of arrogance almost equal to that of Wayne himself, Kerry thought, her eyes taking in the haughty lines of Rowena's mouth and jaw.

Suddenly recalling a conversation she'd had with Mick, Kerry dwelt on it for a space. When Mick had hinted at a deeper relationship than that of secretary and boss existing between Rowena and Wayne, Kerry had instantly reminded him of his assertion that Wayne was immeasurably bored by women, and that he was not the marrying kind.

"True," Mick had agreed, "women do bore him. Also, I'd wager all I have that he'll never allow himself to be caught in the marriage net – nevertheless, he's human and, you must admit, has all the appearance of a very virile male. Can you imagine his living without the normal pleasures of life?" Kerry had only blushed, whereupon Mick had laughed and teased but gone on to embarrass her even further by saying, "Whatever his opinion of women might be he appreciates their uses, and as Rowena Blakely has all the sex appeal any man could desire, plus the fact that she's on the spot – she lives at Wayne's house – I can't see Wayne living the life of a celibate, especially as Rowena obviously finds him attractive. She wouldn't refuse his advances, that's for sure, and there are those who believe she'll get him in the end, although I personally don't think she has a chance."

With this conversation in mind, Kerry turned her head to look at Wayne. Deep in conversation with his friends, he would smile now and then and, fascinated by the transformation, Kerry grudgingly admitted he was the handsomest man she had ever met – and the most striking specimen of manhood she had ever seen. There was no doubt at all that to look on Wayne Harvey was to look on an exception in the world of men. She continued to stare at his finely-chiselled profile; he was smiling quietly over something that had been said ... and suddenly a strange force gripped Kerry, a force both powerful and disturbing.

A slantways glance from Wayne brought a wave of colour to her cheeks, and his dark brows shot up in a gesture of mild enquiry which was far more disconcerting than any show of dislike or contempt could have been. Swiftly averting her head, Kerry took up her wineglass, staring at its contents with quite unnecessary concentration, while instinctively she felt Rowena's eyes on her, and knew the girl was thoroughly enjoying her discomfiture.

But Rowena was not amused when, Clive having got up to dance with his wife, Wayne looked at Kerry and said,

"Would you care to dance, Miss Fairclough?"

If Rowena was taken aback it was nothing to Kerry's reaction. She started visibly, then stared, unable to believe Wayne had risen and was standing there, waiting for her to get to her feet.

Wordlessly she fell into step with him, her heart thumping so madly she felt he must surely hear it – or even feel it, for suddenly she was drawn close to him, as a young couple, so engrossed with each other that they were oblivious of anyone else on the floor, almost collided with them.

Kerry was not left long in doubt as to the reason for Wayne's asking her to dance with him.

"So you're still in Barbados." The fury that he'd been forced to conceal was now portrayed in the look he flashed at her. "What's the idea?"

"It's obvious I'm on the island. I didn't think it necessary to ask your permission to remain here." The retort was out before Kerry stopped to think, and a dark spread of colour infused her partner's face.

"I asked you what the idea was," he snapped, and although another sarcastic rejoinder fought for utterance Kerry was more guarded this time. Increased antagonism between them must be avoided if it were at all possible.

"I don't know what you mean, Mr. Harvey."

"If you're cherishing any hope of seeing my niece then you can get that right out of your head."

She caught her breath, wondering what he would say were he to know that she and Avril had already met twice, and that another meeting had been arranged for the following Wednesday.

"I suppose it's my own fault that you misjudge me," she said with an unhappy sigh. "I know now that I should have written to you and not to Avril. Nevertheless, as you chose to keep her letters from her you should have written to me explaining that Avril was in ignorance of her real parentage." Kerry looked up at him, half hoping to see some slight softening of his expression, but at the mention of Avril's parentage dark fury entered his eyes and he seemed to forget Kerry's reproach against himself.

"For your information my niece was deeply distressed by your disclosure! In fact, she was actually ill for several days."

"I'm sorry – really sorry," returned Kerry, her eyes shading with regret. "Had I known the true position I'd never even have come to Barbados –"

"I don't believe you," he interrupted harshly. "Somehow, you had discovered Avril was a wealthy heiress and you came here for the specific purpose of getting money out of her." There was so much truth in what he said that Kerry blushed hotly, trying to speak but quite unable to do so. She was suddenly distraught, upset beyond measure at having given herself away – and really in so misleading a manner. Would the day ever dawn when he would understand? she wondered, dismally convinced that it never would. "I knew it!" Wayne declared, taking in her flushed cheeks before she hung her head. And then he added, in a much softer voice, "I might as well tell you that it would have been quite impossible. I happen to have full control of Avril's money and she has only what I allow her."

A long silence followed. Kerry could not concentrate on her steps and several times she trod on her partner's toes.

"Can we get off this floor?" she asked miserably at length. "I – I want to go back to the others."

"You're not going back to the others until I've had a talk to you!" And instead of leading her to their table, as Kerry would have wished, he guided her towards the door and within seconds she found herself walking beside him, vaguely aware of the star-sprinkled sky where lazy scudding cloudlets glowed with a silver luminescence stolen from the moon.

Kerry glanced up at him; saw the flint-like hardness of his eyes, the compression of his mouth – and as she had not the least desire to remain with him she stopped, determined to return to the others.

"Charles –" she began, and was sharply interrupted.

"I daresay he'll survive without your company for the next few minutes!"

Anger brought two bright little spots of colour to Kerry's cheeks. She stood still as he moved away; he stopped, took a couple of strides towards her and the next moment her arm was taken and she was once again being propelled unceremoniously along, although the grip on her arm, while firm and inescapable, was not nearly so hurtful as on that previous occasion.

"There's a bench over there –" Wayne gestured with his hand in the direction of some trees. Arriving at the bench, he made another gesture – an imperious flick of his fingers which was an order for her to sit down.

"I don't want –" Kerry got no further. She was pushed on to the bench, trembling a little, and very close to tears.

"Now," said Wayne crisply as he sat down some distance from her so that he could turn and look at her, "we'll talk!"

"Wh-what about?" Kerry evaded, living again through that humiliating experience when he had thrown her out of his house.

"You and Avril, naturally –"

"You now believe we really are sisters?" she interrupted breathlessly.

He ignored the question, yet Kerry took this as an admission that he had in fact now accepted her for what she really was.

"First of all, I want to know why you're still on the island?"

"I hadn't the money for the return fare to England – as I told you – and so I'm having to work."

"You really did come here with only your single fare?" He shook his head in disgust and went on tersely, "Was it your intention ever to return to England?"

"But of course," she answered in some surprise. "I have a – I had a job there."

"And how did you expect to get home?"

Kerry twisted her hands distractedly.

"I can't blame you for being suspicious of me –"

"Answer my question!"

Kerry bent her head.

"I hoped Avril would pay my fare."

A long pause and then,

"What else did you expect to get from Avril?"

Kerry shook her head miserably, refusing to look up.

"You don't understand," she whispered. "But – but it isn't as bad as you think."

"What else did you expect to get from Avril?" he repeated in hard contemptuous tones.

"If I could explain," she began. "If you would be willing to listen?"

"Explain by all means. I'm extremely interested in what you have to say."

She glanced up. Was his voice a trifle softer? So difficult to tell because of the natural cool arrogance of his tones; this she had noticed even when he had been speaking to his friends at the dinner table. His features certainly were not any softer, she noticed, thinking him the most formidable man she had ever met.

"First of all, I really am Avril's sister." She stopped there and waited, but as he made no comment she continued, "I did mean to ask Avril for money, but it was for my other sister, Michelle. You see, she wasn't as fortunate even as I. Her parents are very poor – her father being unemployed. And as her mother has to go out to work Michelle is really little more than a drudge. Her father wants the money for a business, and in exchange he'll let me have Michelle to live with me...." Kerry's voice trailed away into perceptive silence as she watched Wayne's expression.

He didn't believe a word she had uttered.

"Well," he encouraged, "do go on. This is the most interesting tale I've yet heard."

Her colour rose again. She felt she hated him even more for this humiliation than for the previous one.

"I don't really think you want to hear any more," she said tautly at last, but he shook his head.

"On the contrary, I do want to hear more. We haven't yet come to the important matter of the sum you were expecting to get from my niece by this ruse – this hard-luck story concerning some person whom you allege is another sister of yours."

Stung by the injustice of his words, Kerry could take no more. In her anger she forgot that Avril loved and trusted this man, was blind to the fact that an outburst on her own part must inevitably increase Wayne's dislike of her, which in turn would mean that even if accepted by Wayne she would never be a welcome visitor to his home.

"You're the most arrogant, insufferable man I've ever had the misfortune to meet!" she quivered. "You think yourself so clever that you can size up a person at a glance – and perceive a situation. But you've made mistakes on both counts! I'm not a trickster, nor is the situation what you in your self-opinionated pomposity conclude it to be! One day you might discover that you're not such a brilliant detective after all – but you needn't then approach me with an apology, for I want nothing more to do with you ...!"

An awful silence descended as her last words trailed away, Kerry having realized just how foolish they were. Wayne Harvey apologize? A man so bloated with his own pride? It was unthinkable! After a while Kerry ventured a glance at Wayne from under her lashes; even in the moonlight the dark fury in his eyes was easily discernible. She moistened her lips, regretful now of her outburst and fervently wishing she could take everything back.

The silence stretched endlessly. It both surprised and disconcerted her and gradually became a severe test to her nerves – as Wayne probably meant it to, she thought, leaning back in her seat and making a determined effort to forget all about him until he should decide to end the oppressive silence. She was helped by the beauty of her surroundings and by the shadows cast by the trees, which seemed to incite peace. From the dark coral sea the trade-wind breeze blew in, swaying the coconut palms and the whispering casuarina trees, and filling the night air with exotic perfume carried from the flower-strewn garden. Silhouetted against a purple sky were the lovely blue tamarind trees and, closer to, encircled by three mango trees, a small pavilion shone in the moonlight; masses of bougainvillea tumbled down its walls to mingle with mists of sweet-smelling oleander blossoms. The night itself was incredibly brilliant. Crystal clear and intense, the moon floodlit a quivering path from some vague point in the sea to the palm-fringed shore of gleaming white sand.

A voice, soft yet somehow dangerous, brought Kerry back from her tropical paradise to the far less pleasant reality of her formidable companion.

"Now that we've both expressed our opinions of one another, it would appear there is nothing more to say." Wayne rose as he spoke, turning to Kerry, his tall lean figure so close that she caught a breath of some faint elusive scent of after-shave lotion – very reminiscent of wild heather and broad open moorlands scoured by fresh clean winds. Her head tilted back. Their eyes met. Formidable his were and no mistake, with their flint-like hardness and cold expression that was a mingling of contempt and superiority. Kerry noted that lower lip, pursed and sensual; her thoughts strayed to Mick's hint about the relationship existing between Wayne and Rowena, and it required no effort on Kerry's part to decide the relationship did in fact exist. A man of unusual virility, Mick had said, and Kerry mentally agreed with this verdict. "Have you any idea when you'll be leaving the island?" inquired Wayne at last, and Kerry's chin lifted.

"I'll leave when it suits me, Mr. Harvey – and not before."

His eyes glinted dangerously. Kerry wondered if anyone had ever defied this man . . . and if so, how had they fared?

"You can stay as long as you like," he said at last in tones of ice. "But don't you dare try to contact my niece. Understand?"

Kerry swallowed the ball of anger gathering in her throat. How she would love to tell him the truth – that she and Avril had met already – at Avril's request. But of course she dared not; nor dared she argue with him, for surely if she did she would say something indiscreet, something which might give birth to a suspicion in his mind. This must be avoided at all costs and all Kerry said was,

"I understand perfectly, Mr. Harvey." And she hoped that by these specious words of submission she had effectively deceived him.

The summer being the "off" season in Barbados, Kerry was not too busy and Charles did in fact give her another half day free. This meant she could in the ordinary way have spent more time with Avril, but on their next meeting – when Kerry learned to her relief that Avril knew nothing about the encounter between her sister and uncle at Sam Lord's Castle – both girls decided it was far too risky. Yet their decision left Kerry furiously angry with Wayne. What right had he to keep them apart? He had taken this dislike to Kerry and nothing, it seemed, would change his opinion of her. And while this situation existed there was no possible hope of Kerry's being accepted as a member of the family.

For a few days after the dinner at Sam Lord's Castle Charles had been rather cool with Kerry, and she knew moments of fear in case he should decide to give her notice. That he was both curious and jealous was very evident. The curiosity Kerry could understand, because she proffered no explanation of Wayne's apparently strange conduct in taking an unknown girl out into the moonlit garden. The jealousy Kerry did not understand, for she had given Charles no indication whatsoever that she had any feeling for him other than that of an employee. Nevertheless, she did go out to dinner with him again, on several occasions, and on one of these outings they were again seen by Wayne, who this time was alone with his secretary.

The following afternoon, which was Kerry's afternoon off, they were sitting on the lawn of the hotel, drying out after a bathe in the sea, when Charles asked Kerry to go out with him regularly. What his precise intentions were he did not say, and Kerry could not guess; nor did she care, for she had no intention of becoming involved with anyone on the island and she told Charles so.

"For one thing," she added, "I don't know how long I shall be remaining here."

Charles frowned at this.

"Aren't you settled?"

"For a while, yes. But England's my home, and the time will come when I shall wish to return to it." For the present she had to stay, partly because of Avril, but also because of the money she was sending to Mrs. Johnson. Later, when Michelle was older, it was Kerry's intention to return to England and make a home for the two of them, so that Michelle could have some life of her own where she could make friends and, if she wished, find herself a nice boy.

"You'll *wish* to return?" Charles looked sceptically at her. "After sampling this paradise in the sun. I don't see that happening, Kerry. I'm sure you'll settle here – absolutely sure."

"I'm not here to stay indefinitely," Kerry shook her head. "I have a sister at home in England and as soon as she's old enough to come and live with me I shall make a home for us."

"Sister . . . old enough? What do you mean?"

Kerry hesitated, regretting the slip which now made a fuller explanation necessary. However, she did explain without of course mentioning her other sister, living here on the island. What would Charles think, she wondered, if she were to tell him she was the sister of Wayne Harvey's beautiful ward?

"It's damned hard luck on you two," said Charles, frowning as he thought about what Kerry had related to him. "Losing your parents at that age. And then to be separated. It must have been pretty grim for you, being old enough to understand it all, and to know what it was like to have lived as a family."

"It was grim," she nodded, and then, "But one gets over these things, and as for me, I did have good parents who denied me nothing within their means. It's Michelle I'm troubled about and, as I've explained, I want to give her some life of her own."

Charles paused again before he said,

"I do understand your anxiety and determination to get Michelle away, but on the other hand it seems wrong to take her from these people when they're so poor. I mean, she would be working and, therefore, making some contribution to the expenses."

"I've thought it all out. I myself shall contribute to the expenses." Kerry did not tell Charles she was already contributing, but she did tell Avril the next time they met, for Avril herself brought up the subject of Michelle, as she always did, with the wistful expression telling its own tale. "You're dying to meet Michelle, aren't you, Avril?" Kerry asked, watching her sister closely.

Avril turned to her, a hint of sadness in her eyes.

"I'm wanting too much," she said. "I've got you – a

sister of my very own – and even now I'm not satisfied."

"Perhaps," returned Kerry with a little sigh, "I should not have told you about Michelle."

"Of course you should." The wistful expression returned to Avril's face. "Some day I shall meet her, and we'll be friends. If only Uncle Wayne would soften – Oh, yes, he can, Kerry, no matter what you believe to the contrary. He's got this thing about you at present, but he'll come round in the end. I'm sure he will."

Reaching for the teapot, Kerry poured them both more tea.

"He has a thing about me, you say?" Kerry was recalling the strange feeling that had swept over her on the evening she had dined with Wayne and his friends. She had been sitting there, staring at him, when some emotion rose within her, causing her to blush when, on sensing her interest, Wayne had turned a mild stare in her direction.

"He seems to dislike you out of all proportion," replied Avril regretfully. "If only you'd made some different kind of approach – but how were you to know my parents hadn't told me I wasn't theirs?"

"It was unfortunate," Kerry agreed with a small sigh. "Had I known you were in ignorance like that I'd most likely never have come to the island, though, and so we'd never have met."

Avril frowned.

"That would have been awful. No, I'd rather have it this way. It's only for a while – this meeting in secret, I mean. When Uncle Wayne has got over his anger I'll tackle him, saying that I know you're my sister and that I want to see you. He'll let me have my own way," ended Avril with a smile as she noticed the sceptical lift of Kerry's brows.

"Does anyone really ever get their own way with your

75

uncle?" Kerry wanted to know, bringing into mental focus a vision of six foot odd of sinewed male, masterful and autocratic.

"I do – and so does Rowena sometimes. She's not nice to know, really, but Uncle Wayne must like her. He goes out with her and I saw him kissing her once. I sometimes wonder if they'll eventually get married. I'd hate her for an aunt," she added, frowning.

Kerry paused, wondering whether or not to mention her meeting – or perhaps she should say clash – with Avril's uncle a few nights previously. But as Wayne had obviously not said anything to Avril, Kerry decided that she also would keep silent about it.

"They're very friendly, then?" she said, keeping to the subject of Rowena.

"More than friendly." Avril paused, then went on, "I wouldn't speak like this to anyone else except you, of course. But as you're my sister I can say anything – which is marvellous! Oh, I'm so glad I've found you –" Avril broke off, laughing. "I mean of course that I'm glad *you* found *me*."

"So am I." But Kerry's voice was rather sad, for she was thinking of Michelle. "You believe there's a possibility of your uncle marrying Rowena?" she queried at length, as if forced to do so.

"Most people think Uncle Wayne's not the marrying kind, that he's a confirmed bachelor, but he loves children and that seems evidence enough that he'll marry one day. Don't you think so?"

"Not necessarily," returned Kerry after some thought. "Many bachelors love children but aren't all that keen on having any of their own."

"I'm sure Uncle Wayne would like to have children of his own."

Kerry frowned, wondering why the idea of Wayne's

marrying his secretary should seem so distasteful to her. The feeling persisted, hovering in the far recesses of her mind like the unpleasant aftermath of a bad dream.

As usual she and Avril were to leave the café by separate taxis after arranging to meet at the same place the following week.

"Soon we'll be meeting at Uncle Wayne's house," said Avril confidently on getting into her taxi. "I know I should be thankful I'm seeing you every week like this, but it really isn't enough. I'm hoping that very soon Uncle Wayne will ask you to come and live at our house."

Live with Avril. That would be wonderful, but all the same Kerry knew she could never be happy until she had sorted something out for Michelle. If only Wayne would come round perhaps he'd believe her story about Michelle, and allow Avril to put up the money which would procure Michelle's freedom. She would then come to Barbados and they would all be together for a while until Kerry decided to return to England. A reunion of the three of them ... this was what Kerry had planned on inheriting her aunt's money, and if only Wayne could be persuaded to accept Kerry then her one abiding hope would be fulfilled.

Avril was in her taxi and Kerry stood by her own, waving until Avril was lost to view round a bend in the road.

"The Beach Manor Hotel," Kerry smiled at the coloured driver as she made to step into the taxi.

"Yes, missy –"

"You needn't get into that taxi!" The masculine voice, vibrating with suppressed fury, sent an icy shiver down Kerry's spine. "You're not going anywhere at present."

"Mr. Harvey!" Kerry almost stumbled back on to the ground, every vestige of colour draining from her face. "How long – I mean, do you know ...?" What a stupid question! Of course he knew; that expression could almost have meant murder, and instinctively Kerry stepped to one side as, his smouldering gaze still fixed on her white face, Wayne spoke to the taxi driver.

"How much?"

"The lady was going to the Beach Manor Hotel –"

"I said how much!" Wayne's hand was already in his pocket and the money was passed over immediately the man stated his price. "You can go; we don't need you."

"Yes, sir." The man glanced curiously at Kerry before hastily getting into his cab.

It soon disappeared the way Avril's had gone and Kerry found herself alone, on the forecourt of the café, with her sister's irate guardian – Irate? That was a mild description, she decided, noting the trace of whiteness which had appeared under the attractive bronze of his skin, and the slow pulsation of a muscle in his cheek. She thought, "He looks capable of murder," and involuntarily a hand fluttered to her throat. The silent tension becoming unbearable, she was driven to speech.

"You had no right to send my taxi away –"

"Just how long has my niece been deceiving me?" So soft the voice . . . yet still vibrant with wrath. Kerry trembled, scarcely able to articulate words.

"Not l-long – I mean, Avril and I. . . ." Her voice melted away into silence as she realized that the proprietor of the café, having come outside, was standing on the step, watching with curiosity this little scene being enacted on his forecourt. "We've been m-meeting on Wednesdays."

Wayne's mouth went tight; Kerry felt he would dearly love to strike her.

"I asked you how long!"

"Avril –" she began, not intentionally ignoring his question but rather voicing the fear she felt for her sister. In this mood Wayne would be capable of anything, Kerry thought. "What are you going to do – say to her?"

78

"Plenty!" he snapped, and Kerry's nerves fluttered, out of control. Wayne's eyes moved to the man on the step and then, gesturing to an unseen place at the back of the café, "Into my car!" The order, rapped out as if to a servant, brought Kerry's head up with a jerk despite the wild condition of her nerves. "And at the first sign of argument," said Wayne in dangerously quiet tones, "you'll be put in the car by force."

"Force?" The one word escaped her in a rush of disbelief as her lovely eyes flew to his. "You'd f-force m-me?"

"Let's not be melodramatic. Into the car; it's round at the back."

Prudently Kerry obeyed, because she really did not have much fight in her. This man was too overpowering, too dominant, and she sped along beside him as he strode towards the corner of the building.

CHAPTER V

ONCE in the car Wayne drove in silence, while Kerry sat beside him, aware of breadfruit trees and mangoes flying past as Wayne headed for some destination unknown to Kerry. Why didn't he speak? she wondered, feeling as if she were confined in some inescapable net, awaiting complete annihilation. Silently she admonished herself for not putting up some resistance to Wayne's intimidating behaviour. How could she have meekly allowed herself to be so peremptorily ordered into the car and driven away like this? What stupid and unnecessary fear had gripped her during those vital moments when she could so easily have found safe refuge in a return to the café? But her lack of resistance had been the result of several factors:

alarm at Wayne's discovery, fear for Avril, and of course the almost paralysing effect of Wayne's forceful personality. A word of command from Wayne Harvey and it would seem one was quite unable to offer even the smallest measure of defiance.

Automatically glancing through the window, Kerry saw that they were travelling along the western shore of the island – the "platinum coast" whose tranquil sands were washed by the limpid Caribbean. To the right the ubiquitous sugar-cane swept over vast tracts of undulating land, the arrows of greenish-grey quivering and bending in the breeze. Among the sugar-canes brightly-clothed labourers sang as they worked and now and then one or other of them would lift a dusky hand and wave; but it was not until the great colonnaded house came into the distant view that Kerry realized that the plantation through which they drove did in fact belong to Wayne.

"Where are we going?" The question was asked in rather breathless tones, for it suddenly occurred to Kerry that Wayne was taking her to his house.

"To my office – where we can talk undisturbed," replied Wayne shortly, dashing Kerry's newly-risen hopes.

"Your office?" she quivered, afraid all at once because she disliked intensely the idea of finding herself alone with a man whose hatred for her was so intense.

A swift turn of Wayne's dark head in her direction and then,

"Where did you think we were going?" Curt the tones and faintly sardonic. His eyes were fixed on an Italianate pillared urn visible through the mass of tropical trees and shrubs surrounding his lovely eighteenth-century mansion standing on a slight elevation, its newly-constructed summer house gleaming in the sunshine, for it was built of coral, which had a beautiful natural patina.

"I thought we might be going to your house," Kerry

answered at length in a rather flat little voice.

"My house, eh?" Dark brows lifted. "Still hoping, it would seem."

"You know I'm Avril's sister," Kerry said quietly, ignoring his faintly satirical response.

"If you are, I still don't believe your motives in coming here were honourable."

So he had admitted it at last; but strangely Kerry derived no satisfaction.

"Why do you condemn my motives out of hand like this?"

"Because I know your sort, that's why." He swung off the road on to a strip of concrete fronting a low building. "I've met them before, remember." He stopped the car and turned his head. Kerry gave a helpless shrug. How did one scale the barrier of inflexibility such as this? Did anyone ever reach the man? Even as she asked the question it struck her that Avril had most certainly reached him. It was a miracle! Had Kerry on her arrival discovered that Avril went in terror of her guardian the situation would have been more in line with Wayne's character as Kerry now knew it ... but Avril did not go in terror of him. On the contrary, she spoke of him with deep affection, and said with firm confidence that sooner or later he would come round, accepting Kerry and inviting her to his home.

Wayne slid from the car and took a key from his pocket. Kerry slammed her door with unnecessary force, just to remind him of his lack of manners in not opening it for her.

The action produced a frown of annoyance, nothing more.

"In here." The door was flung open and Kerry passed in front of him, finding herself in a sumptuously furnished office which had been fitted out with no regard to

81

cost. "Sit down." Wayne indicated a chair, but Kerry preferred to stand.

She had felt, during that silent drive, that his fury had subsided, but looking up and encountering his smouldering gaze Kerry realized Wayne had merely been keeping that fury in check. Its release was imminent and, in complete contrast to her intended resistance to intimidation, a trembling hand fluttered automatically to her throat, for without doubt Wayne Harvey looked quite ready to murder her.

"Is it necessary? What you have to say can't take many minutes." She had to show some spirit, Kerry determinedly told herself, otherwise this man would completely swamp her. "Perhaps I could put a question first? Might I ask how you came to be spying on Avril and me? – I expect you were spying," she added as an afterthought.

His lips went tight, and she saw the slow clenching movement of his hand.

"Be careful," he warned gratingly. "You're here to answer questions, not ask them. Keep that in mind if you don't want this interview to be too unpleasant."

Kerry's blood boiled; how could she even be civil to the man? And yet she must, for Avril's sake. Wayne also remained standing, but she did not look at him. Her mind at the moment was occupied with the question she had just put to him. Yet on thinking about her meetings with Avril, Kerry felt she should have known that Wayne Harvey would sooner or later come to hear of them. Barbados was a small island; the workers would have relations everywhere and in all probability one of the taxi drivers, knowing Avril by sight, had a brother or cousin working for Wayne in some capacity or other. Word would soon get round, and eventually it had come to Wayne's ears that his ward was meeting another girl every Wednesday at a café which, in the ordinary way, would not be plush enough for Avril to frequent. Yes, the explanation was simple, as was Wayne's presence at the café. Deciding to come, he had sat in his car, at the back of the café, while she and Avril were inside. Why hadn't he entered and confronted them? Kerry wondered, and then realized that Wayne would never cause a sensation which could – and certainly would – be talked about all over the island.

Kerry's drifting thoughts were interrupted by the harsh tones of her companion demanding to know how long she and Avril had been seeing one another. On being informed that it was six weeks since their first meeting Wayne exploded.

"Six weeks! Then you were already meeting regularly when I forbade you to make any attempt to contact my niece?" Kerry nodded and in a hollow little voice said yes, that was correct. "All this time Avril has been deceiving me –" He broke off, plainly unable to accept this fact. The fury in his face was terrifying and Kerry steeled herself for what must surely come. "First you inflict untold misery on my niece," he almost snarled, "and now you encourage her to deceit! Do you realize," he continued, taking a step which brought him uncomfortably close to Kerry, "that Avril never once deceived either her parents or me until you exerted your influence on her! Whose idea was it that you should meet?" he demanded, and the very fact of Kerry's hesitation answered him. However, in her ignorance Kerry failed to grasp this and in an effort to shield Avril she began to lie.

"It was my idea, Mr. Harvey –"

"It was?" An odd glance now and a much quieter tone ... but dangerous for all that, and Kerry suddenly had an urge to run from him, an urge which required very little suppressing, for obviously she would not get very far. "Your idea? And how did you get in touch with her?"

In her haste and confusion Kerry could think of only one reply to that and she said she had telephoned Avril, asking her to arrange a meeting.

"You telephoned her, did you?" The question appeared unnecessary, but Kerry obligingly said,

"Yes, I telephoned her."

"Miss Fairclough, you're a liar! Ever since your visit to my house someone has listened to all incoming telephone calls, even though I expected you'd leave the island. If I haven't been there myself I've left instructions for someone else to listen in to them."

"You actually spied on her." Kerry's voice was so low that she wondered if he had heard. He certainly did not reply to her question.

"So now perhaps I can have the truth. It was *Avril* who contacted *you*, wasn't it?"

Kerry caught her lip between her teeth, raising her eyes to search his face.

"Mr. Harvey – you won't punish Avril?" she whispered, blinking rapidly, for tears pricked the back of her eyes. Why had she ever been left that money? she whispered fiercely. Why – when it was to bring so much heartache and trouble both to herself and others? Wayne was standing over her, his gaze narrowed and denunciatory. Ignoring her plea concerning Avril, he once again subjected Kerry to a scathing invective, reminding her again that Avril had never practised deceit until Kerry had come along and exerted a bad influence on her.

"Let me tell you," he continued wrathfully, "that it's only the law which prevents me from meting out some fitting punishment. Women like you ought to be whipped!"

The blood rushed to Kerry's face, but his words did serve to infuriate her to the point of retaliation.

"No doubt your sadistic desires – of which your treat-

84

ment of me was an illustration – comes from your slave-trading forebears! What a pity times have changed and that such pleasures as beating your servants are denied you!"

Silence followed. Had she touched him on a raw spot? Kerry wondered, watching his face for some sign of emotion. She must have, for of course his ancestors had enriched themselves at the expense of the slaves – men, women and children whose very existence was a living hell under their rapacious white masters. Wayne's house and garden, his plantation, and in fact his entire wealth must originally have been the result of slave-labour. Kerry continued to watch Wayne's face; it was grim and taut, but his expression had an enigmatical quality that told her nothing. Yet Kerry waited, ready for a wrathful outburst, but to her surprise he reacted very differently, regaining command of the situation in a manner only Wayne Harvey could. He totally ignored her vindictive allusion to the inherited vices of his ancestors, obviously considering it unworthy even of the smallest comment.

"As I remarked, Miss Fairclough, were it not for the law I should see that you were fittingly punished for the havoc you've caused; and if it weren't for my principles I'd also see that you were paid to leave this island –"

"Paid? By you?" Kerry tossed her head in the air. "Mr. Harvey, you're quite insufferable! What, might I ask, gives you this idea that I'd accept payment to leave Barbados?"

His brows shot up; the fury hitherto in evidence was suddenly replaced by mere contempt.

"You came here with the intention of persuading my niece to part with money, so it's reasonable to assume you'd be equally willing to accept money to leave. However, as I've implied, bribery of this nature is alien to my principles and therefore I'm not offering you money.

However, your employer is a friend of mine and I shall see that you're very soon out of a job."

"You'd get me dismissed?" Kerry stared, and in a rush of conviction she knew for sure that Charles would be influenced by his friend, especially as Kerry had flatly refused to enter into any kind of relationship with him. "You believe you have the right to keep two sisters apart?"

"Under the present circumstances – yes, I do. In my opinion Avril is better off without you." He looked squarely at Kerry. "By your own admission you came here intending to get money from her – this in itself proves that Avril must be protected from you."

Kerry bit her lip.

"Mr. Harvey –" She looked up at him, on the verge of tears. "I don't deserve this – really I don't. My intentions were honourable – in the main. Perhaps I did have visions of getting money from Avril, but as I said it was only in order to help my other sister." Kerry continued to stare at him as she added, "You wouldn't listen – you never listen to anything I say –"

"On the contrary," he interposed, "I've listened both with interest and patience to all you've had to say."

Blushing at the sarcasm in his tones, Kerry said fiercely,

"Very well, you listen, but you're not affected. You've branded me a trickster and nothing I can do or say will change your opinion of me." She paused a moment to allow him to speak, but all at once he seemed tired of the conversation – bored even, yet Kerry added, a sudden note of pleading in her voice, "Mr. Harvey, my remaining on the island can't inconvenience you in any way, while it means a great deal to me ... and to others. Please don't get me the sack." To beg in this way went against the grain, naturally, but Kerry's thoughts were with Michelle. She must continue to send the money, otherwise it must appear that she, Kerry, was full of promises

86

she could not fulfil, for this would be the second time she had failed Michelle. Should she tell Wayne that she sent money to Michelle's parents every week? But no; Kerry had proof and enough that whatever she said to Wayne would never be believed. "You won't get me the sack?" she faltered, tears misting her vision. "If – if I promise not to see Avril again –" Kerry stopped. How could she make such a promise when she had only just found her sister? Already they loved one another and had been looking forward to the day when they could meet openly. "I c-can't. . . ." To her dismay Kerry burst into tears. She put her face into her hands, uncaring that she disgraced herself before Wayne Harvey. He neither knew nor cared about the anguish through which she had passed since inheriting her aunt's money. And if ever he did come to know Kerry was sure he would remain coldly unaffected by the knowledge. "You're heartless – you don't possess any emotion at all!" Kerry spoke wildly, opening her handbag and searching for an elusive handkerchief among letters and make-up and other odds and ends. "You're incapable of emotion, or feelings or – or – understanding! It's no wonder you're not married – you wouldn't know what to do –!" She broke off, horrified. How on earth had she come to say a thing like that? she asked herself, aware of his startled gasp. The handkerchief came to light at last and Kerry held it to her face, hot with embarrassment and mortification at the unthinking rush of words which were so utterly irrelevant. She kept her head bent as she lowered the handkerchief; but she was not to be allowed to avoid his gaze, for with a most uncharacteristic gesture Wayne put a finger under her chin and tipped her head right back, his expression clearly portraying his imperviousness to her tears.

"And what," he drawled with a sort of lazy humour, "makes you so sure of that?"

At a complete loss, as much owing to the unexpected lack of roughness in his touch as to the question itself, Kerry could only stare wordlessly at him for a long moment, conscious of an unaccountable wild confusion of her senses. "I asked you a question, Miss Fairclough," Wayne smoothly reminded her, retaining his hold on her chin.

Kerry shook her head, wondering why it should feel as if she had just partaken of some potent drug.

"I shouldn't have said it," came her almost inaudible reply at last. Her great eyes were still filmed with moisture; but they were also wide and unhappy, and her lovely lips quivered in the most attractive and alluring way. Wayne's eyes flickered strangely, then became fixed on her face, curious and exploratory. The stillness pervading the room seemed fraught with tension as the silent moments passed and Wayne became immersed in thought. There appeared to be some intangible transformation in his manner towards her ... it was as if he saw her in a new and more interesting light. Kerry stirred uneasily, and her eyes strayed to the window. The scene outside was beautiful and exotic – the waving hemisphere of sugar-cane in which the labourers sang and worked; the distant colony of palm-thatched huts in which they dwelt. Mahogany trees shaded a nearby terrace whose gleaming coral pillars were swathed in poinsettias and hibiscus. Kerry's wandering gaze absorbed the distant infinity of graceful Royal palms, their smooth, perfectly cylindrical trunks towering to a phenomenal height and their enormous corolla of leaves forming a dark mysterious mass against a cloud-flecked tropical sky. Draped in sunlight, the coral sea danced rhythmically towards the palm-fringed shore of silver sand.

A restless movement in the room brought Kerry's attention from the dazzling panorama outside; Wayne's

88

face was a study of indecision which sent her pulses fluttering in some indefinable way. Kerry had the odd impression that a vague idea was forming in his mind. She held his gaze for a long moment. How inordinately attractive he was! From the first Kerry was forced to admit this. Tall and erect, lithe and slender, Wayne Harvey possessed a bearing as proud and as majestic as any king. Suddenly, with the swift unexpected jerk of her heart as the only warning, Kerry was swept into the whirlpool of his magnetism, trapped in a spell that set her captured heart racing and drove her mind into a stream of wild confusion. Delicate colour fluctuated in her cheeks and a brightness touched her eyes that had nothing to do with the film of tears still covering them. Wayne's shrewd gaze was still fixed upon her . . . missing nothing. . . .

"So I'm incapable of emotion, am I?" Wayne's voice was oddly gentle, reminding Kerry of the satisfied purr of a cat when playing with a mouse. "And if I were married I wouldn't know what to do?" His hand dropped to his side as, hot with embarrassment, Kerry twisted away and stood some distance from him, over by the desk. "You know, Miss Fairclough," came the gentle drawl once more, "I've a mind to let you see whether or not I'm incapable of emotion."

Kerry's eyes flew to his as her heart jerked. What did he mean? And what an unexpected situation in which to find herself. On being brought here – to talk undisturbed, Wayne had said – Kerry expected to feel the lash of his fury to which she had just been subjected; she had also half expected Wayne to forbid any further meetings between her and Avril . . . but a scene such as this had never remotely touched her horizon. She stared at him intently. Nothing in those lazy grey eyes to match his subtle threat, yet Kerry somehow gained the impression that despite his rather abstracted look he was in fact more than a little piqued at Kerry's impulsive and unthinking slur on his manhood, and of course this was understandable. What on earth had made her utter those ridiculous words?

From being piqued Wayne surprisingly became amused. Misled by the laugh which broke the silence, Kerry was edged into safety again as she looked up into a face that had undergone a miraculous transformation. Wayne was human all at once, and an involuntary smile broke on Kerry's lips.

"Yes ... I've a good mind to give you a small demonstration...." His laugh faded, and so did Kerry's smile. Too late her nerves sprang to the alert and she had taken only a couple of steps towards the door when she was caught and jerked back. "A statement like that impels me to disprove it."

"Let me go –!" Kerry's protest was smothered by his kiss and although she instinctively tried to struggle from the hardness enveloping her she soon desisted, admitting the futility of her efforts. Wayne held her as if she were no stronger than a baby.

"Well ...?" After an eternity he held her from him, looking into her flushed face with an expression of sardonic amusement. He seemed to be waiting – probably for the outraged remonstrance which by right Kerry should already be directing at him, but, inconceivably, she seemed for the moment to have lost the power of speech. "Are you now ready to take it back?"

"Take it b-back?" she repeated huskily. Her lips were bruised and swollen, her whole body on fire. Wayne had certainly achieved his object in giving the lie to her foolishly-spoken words about his inability to feel emotion.

"The insult, my dear," he returned softly. "Take it back ... or else...."

For the present the threat went unheard. Shaken to the depths, Kerry closed her eyes, ashamed of the response

Wayne had at last drawn from her – a response that had been a long while in coming, for Kerry's determined resistance was strong. But inevitably the point of surrender was reached – and Kerry now knew that Wayne would never have released her until he had broken her strength.

"If – if there's nothing more to say," faltered Kerry at last, "perhaps you'll take me to some place where I can get a taxi." Her accents were jerky, the result of heightened emotions. The power of this man was incredible

"Look at me," he commanded, ignoring her request.

Kerry's lids fluttered open, but she kept her head averted. Wayne lifted her chin and looked, with a mixture of perception and triumph, into eyes that were still smoky with the dying ashes of awakened desire.

"You haven't obeyed my request." The one careless finger keeping her head up seemed to be illustrative of the supreme arrogance of the man – and of his mastery.

"Obeyed?" Kerry tried to infuse some hauteur into her voice, but failed utterly to make any impression on Wayne, whose mouth merely curved with a sort of satirical mockery as he said, in a very soft tone,

"I insist that you take back your insult."

Her eyes flashed then, and her small fists clenched. Wayne's eyes moved slowly downwards from her face to her hands and his smile deepened. What a pompous, insufferable, self-opinionated man he was! Fervently she wished she had the strength and the courage to strike him a wounding blow.

"I've already admitted I shouldn't have said it."

"And now you *know* you shouldn't have said it." Half statement, half question. Kerry made no reply and the pressure on her arms increased slightly. A warning? Kerry decided it was and her mouth trembled. Her eyes, supplicating and persuasive, beseeched him to release her.

Wayne caught his breath, ignoring the silent plea.

"If you continue to look at me like this –" The sudden touch of that sensuous lower lip on her mouth was like the gentle caress of a clean cool breeze ... but seconds later her lips were again fully possessed and the gentleness was drowned in a tide of passion and desire on which Kerry was swept helplessly along even while feebly striving to set up some resistance. Breathless when for the second time he held her from him, she was staggered by his unruffled air of calm serenity.

"Take it back," he murmured gently. "Be honest for once in your life."

Be honest for once! Must he always fling insults at her? Retaliation was called for, but Kerry was still profoundly shaken both by his treatment of her and by her earlier awareness of Wayne's attraction.

"I'm sorry I said that," she managed presently, deciding that an indignant outcry could only result in prolonging this conversation, and this she had not the least desire to do. "I was upset, and angry. . . ." Kerry tailed off lamely, and looked up into his unmoving countenance.

"I asked for a retraction, not an apology." The gentle reminder had the effect of infuriating Kerry. Every time she met this man she was subjected to some form of humiliation. If she didn't make a stand he'd eventually have her grovelling in the dust!

"Why should I take it back! You've treated me abominably –"

"Abominably?"

"The – the way you've just – just kissed m-me," she said in choking accents. "How dare you treat me as if – as if –" A warm flush of embarrassment took the place of further words. Wayne laughed and said, flinging her a humorous glance,

"You liked it well enough, apparently."

"Liked it!" echoed Kerry furiously, not stopping to probe her mind for the truth. "I hated it! – *hated* it, Mr. Harvey, so you can take that satisfied and triumphant smirk off your face!"

His laugh rang out again, a laugh of sheer amusement. Kerry's face flamed and the slow curling of her fingers was evidence enough of what she would like to do to him. Strangle him? That was too humane. He should be slowly tortured!

"Totally unconvincing," he said when he had recovered. "I've yet to meet a woman who's averse to male attention."

"Mr. Harvey," she said in suffocated tones, "there might be a good deal of truth in what you say – but in my case it happens to depend on the particular male! *Your* attention can hardly provide me with enjoyment. I think you'll agree about that!"

Surprisingly, a little twinkle of amusement played about Wayne's eyes.

"I do agree it hasn't been exactly pleasant for you up till now, but you could hardly expect it, could you? However, I still maintain – from observation," he added on a distinctly humorous note, "that you thoroughly enjoyed our little interlude just now. Enjoyed – er – learning that I could in fact feel emotion ... and arouse it, Miss Fairclough."

Seething, Kerry could only stare speechlessly at him and he continued, suddenly impatient of the digression,

"I'm still waiting for you to take back that insult." He paused; Kerry's eyes dropped and, staring at her hands, she found herself fumbling for something to say, for instinct warned her that Wayne would coerce her into a complete retraction of her impulsive statement. Deciding it were better to get the wretched business over and done with, she lifted her head and, in a voice so low it was almost inaudible, she said,

"I t-take it all back, Mr. Harvey."

A strange silence followed; Kerry saw that underlip curve with the hint of a smile ... but where was the triumph, the smug sneer of satisfaction which should have spread across that handsome face?

"You are very wise, Miss Fairclough," was all he said, allowing a moment of silence to elapse in case any response was forthcoming from Kerry. But she remained wordlessly staring in front of her and he then said, "I'll take you back to your hotel."

"If you take me to a taxi, that will do."

"I'll take you all the way."

Kerry swallowed, ready to break into tears again. And the reason for this was so strange, for why should she want to cry just because, all of a sudden, Wayne had become quite human? – losing the customary harshness which had hitherto characterized his attitude towards her, and in fact speaking rather softly, just as if he had suddenly ceased to dislike her. The idea brought a fluttering to her heart and nerves and she said without thinking,

"Mr. Harvey, please don't get me the sack." Her lovely eyes were wide, entreating. Wayne, on his way to the door, stopped and turned, a frown between his eyes.

"For the present, Miss Fairclough, I'll leave things as they are."

"Oh ... thank you!" A small uncertain pause and then, "Avril? Can she – can we see each other sometimes?"

The frown deepened.

"I'll see," was as far as Wayne would go, and with that Kerry had to be satisfied.

CHAPTER VI

With the complete return to clear-headed thinking Kerry's self-disgust grew. What were Wayne's thoughts? she wondered, casting him a sideways glance but learning nothing from his carved set profile. He was driving straight ahead, his long slender hands merely resting on the steering-wheel of the car. Was he thinking about her, despising her even more than previously – and for an altogether different reason? She had enjoyed his lovemaking, he had firmly asserted, and although it would have been far more comfortable to forget both his words and his actions, Kerry found herself re-living those moments when, her struggles assisting in her own defeat, she had been robbed even of the power to remain resolutely inert. Having decided to teach her a lesson, Wayne had ruthlessly pursued a masculine course of temptation which he knew would inevitably break her resistance. Angry and mortified though she was by his success, Kerry was at the same time honest enough to admit that the experience of surrender had been far from unpleasant. Stimulated both by his magnetism and his dominance, she was swept into a realm of impalpable emotions where her only tangible impression was a confusion of excitement and exquisite fear. Reasoning dispassionately, Kerry was inclined to believe there had been an easy surrender on her part rather than a hard-won victory on his. Why had she not put up a greater resistance – imbued as she was with so strong a dislike of him? She glanced sideways and upwards. Could any woman resist such a man? She very much doubted it; he was altogether too attractive, too dangerously masculine, she decided, drawing a breath of thankfulness that she would never again be in a position where he could tempt her. But an immediate backward swing of memory brought the reminder that, even prior to that scene of physical contact, her emotions had been profoundly disturbed by the devastating charm of the man who, by all that was logical, she should be hating with the darkest venom. Did she hate him? With a sort of subconscious reaction she evaded an answer to that. Dislike she most certainly felt, considering him far too arrogant and imbued with an inflated sense of his own superiority. Added to these undesirable characteristics were those of domination and mastery. What a life he would give any woman who might be misguided enough to marry him!

Mick had said with sure conviction that he would never marry; and Kerry could only feel that a man like Wayne Harvey should remain a bachelor, for she could not imagine him being faithful to one particular woman all his life.

"Here we are." Kerry woke from her musings to the fact that they were already travelling along the wide approach to the front of the hotel, driving under a leafy canopy of interlocking trees through which slanting sunbeams intermittently threw shafts of gold into the car. Away to the west the sun trailed its downward course to the sea, and the fleet of cumulus clouds driven by the trade winds became a miracle of changing colour, with pearl melting into lilac and then breathtakingly into flame and bronze interlaced with saffron and translucent coppergold. "Have you confided in your employer?" inquired Wayne as he made a wide sweep on reaching the head of the long avenue of limes.

"Confided?"

"Told him all your business. Women usually seize the first opportunity of becoming expansive. I find them deplorably lacking in restraint." Kerry received a quizzical glance as Wayne added in some amusement, "I was referring only to their tongues, of course." The very manner of delivery seemed to be a contradiction of the statement; to Kerry it contained a subtle allusion to the scene recently enacted and she turned away, unwilling to provide him with further amusement by allowing him to read her expression. A soft laugh escaped him nevertheless, and Kerry's temper flared.

"You obviously have a very low opinion of women, Mr. Harvey, but as that opinion is of no interest whatsoever to me you waste time in voicing it!"

"I merely stated a fact," he drawled, appearing faintly bored all at once. "Did you tell Charles why you came here?"

"It so happens," she replied in tones of ice, "that I am not one of those women who seize the first opportunity of becoming expansive! I can usually manage to keep my private affairs to myself."

Another laugh from Wayne as, braking slowly, he brought the car gently to a standstill outside the main entrance of the hotel.

"Then I congratulate you, Miss Fairclough." Although sarcasm and amusement edged his tones he was no longer hostile towards her and, surprised, Kerry twisted round again and stared at him. His head was turned in her direction; his eyes became intently watchful the moment they met hers.

"I – don't understand you," she murmured impulsively and with an automatic little shake of her head.

"There isn't the slightest reason why you should, Miss Fairclough." A flick of his finger and the door flew open. Easing his long body from the car, he moved to the other side with the intention of opening Kerry's door for her, but Charles was before him, much to Kerry's dismay. She had hoped to avoid seeing Charles until after Wayne's departure.

Charles glanced from Wayne to Kerry in wordless silence, although the lift of his fair brows was a question in itself. Wayne merely said,

"I gave Miss Fairclough a lift," and pointedly ignored his friend's interrogating gesture. Obviously that was the only explanation Charles was to receive – at least from Wayne. But Kerry had a feeling that, later, she herself would be questioned by her employer. Few women rode in Wayne Harvey's car, and Kerry could not help but wonder at the odd way in which Charles was looking at her. Was he thinking things he shouldn't? The idea brought the colour to her cheeks; Wayne raised an eyebrow questioningly, but a moment later he turned to Charles. "How's business?" he asked conversationally.

"A little quiet," replied Charles, his eyes still on Kerry. "I shall be full in a fortnight's time, though."

"Full?" echoed Kerry, diverted. "There's the package tour from England, I know, but that won't fill the hotel."

"I've received two bookings today, one for a party of ten and the other for eight. We also have a honeymoon couple coming in, so that just about fills us up."

"Honeymoon couple?" No doubting the touch of sardonic amusement in Wayne Harvey's voice. "Another poor devil making a fool of himself."

Charles laughed at that.

"Always the cynic. One of these days, Wayne, you're going to eat those words. What makes you think you're immune, anyway?"

"I've a built-in protection – plus a good deal of foresight and common sense." His grey eyes travelled to Kerry, and settled on her face. "It wouldn't do for everyone to be like me, though," he admitted goodhumouredly. "Or the race would very soon die out." Kerry made no response, mainly because once again her mind was occupied with the recent happenings in Wayne Harvey's office, and

98

with the troublesome recurring memories of the earlier revelation that she was by no means impervious to the intense masculinity of her sister's guardian.

He was chatting with Charles and, excusing herself, Kerry went inside and up to her room. On the dressing-table were two letters; eagerly she picked them up. One from Michelle and the other from Irene. Irene was getting married in a fortnight's time and had already given up the tenancy of the flat, having moved in with her parents for a week or two prior to the wedding. Kerry opened her sister's letter first and as she read down the pages a slow frown gathered between her eyes. On the surface the letter was cheerful and certainly newsy. Why, then, this odd sensation of foreboding? – this intangible un-easiness and suspicion that all was not well with her sister?

Thoughtfully Kerry folded the pages, then opened them out again. No mention of what Michelle had done with the personal spending money Kerry sent her. . . . Nor had there been any mention of it last week, Kerry recalled. Before that Michelle wrote expansive and eager descriptions of what she had done with her money. Kerry shook her head. Nothing to worry about. Michelle had not thought it necessary to explain what she did with her money. At first it was a novelty to have any, but now she was used to it and had not bothered to go into details as to how she had spent it.

Shaking off her misgivings – for they really had no sub-stance – Kerry picked up the other letter, her eyes widen-ing with surprise and pleasure as she swiftly went through it.

After beginning by thanking Kerry for her wedding present Irene continued,

"You'll be very surprised at my news. As you know, we weren't having a honeymoon as we've had such an expense with the alterations to the house, but last week Aunt Chrissy had a win on the pools and offered us a honeymoon out of it. She wanted it to be something special and of course I thought of the Caribbean – one does, doesn't one, for things like honeymoons! And thinking of the Caribbean I naturally thought of you – so we managed to get in on a package tour going to Barbados – a cancellation, it was – and what do you think! We'll be staying at the Beach Manor Hotel! I just can't believe it, a fabulous honeymoon, all free, and seeing you into the bargain. What a rush life is at present, though. Last-minute shopping and all the rest. Have some news concerning Michelle, but would rather leave it until I see you. Love, Irene."

News concerning Michelle . . . and Irene would rather leave it until they met! Somehow these words of Irene's seemed to justify Kerry's suspicions that all was not well with Michelle, and she felt a quick return of her previous anxiety, an anxiety she could not now shake off. If only Wayne Harvey would act like a human being and listen sympathetically to what she had to say – how simple the whole situation would be. Michelle's happiness would be assured and so would that of Avril and Kerry herself. Kerry wished she could hate him as much as she ought.

What would he say to Avril? she wondered, for some incomprehensible reason feeling convinced that, during the interlude in his office, most of his anger had evaporated, and Kerry was not now unduly troubled about Avril.

Charles invited Kerry out to dinner on the Friday; she accepted and they drove along the rocky Atlantic coast of the island to Sam Lord's Castle. After parking the car Charles suggested a stroll in the grounds before going into the hotel for their meal. He was still puzzled by Wayne's interest in Kerry and although he had not pursued the matter after Wayne left on Wednesday it was obvious by the odd glances he often sent in Kerry's direction that he was both curious and faintly jealous.

And so Kerry was not surprised when, as they walked together through the impressive grounds of the Castle, Charles suddenly broached the subject.

"Wayne Harvey appears to be rather more than ordinarily interested in you." Just a statement, but Charles turned his head interrogatingly. Kerry hesitated and then, lightly,

"I don't know what you mean, Charles? He gave me a lift – which was quite a normal action, seeing that he had a car and I hadn't."

"Normal? You think so? Kerry, Wayne Harvey doesn't give women lifts. If he happens to be out in his car it's more often than not on business. He has very little interest in women at any time, and virtually none at all when he's going about his business."

Kerry turned her head.

"What are you insinuating?" she inquired in a low vibrating tone.

"I'm not insinuating," was the swift, apologetic reply. "But I am puzzled. First, he took you outside when we last dined here, and then he gave you that lift." A pause, but as Kerry offered no comment he added, "His interest puzzles me exceedingly."

That final remark brought a smile to her lips.

"You're not very flattering, Charles – nor very diplomatic."

He raised his brows, evincing no sign at all of contrition.

"Physical attractions pass over Wayne Harvey's head – he rarely has eyes for feminine beauty. This has been proved over and over again." They had reached a bench and Charles invited Kerry to sit down. He took a seat beside her. "A man as rich and attractive as Wayne is always a target, and numerous beautiful females have set their caps at him. As he remarked, he's armed with a built-in protection –"

"Charles," interrupted Kerry softly, "why are you saying all this?"

Another couple were passing them, strolling hand in hand under a tropical moon which must surely have been designed especially for lovers. Charles's eyes followed them until their dark silhouettes merged into a single indistinct shape as they stopped to kiss by the lake. Waiting for him to speak, Kerry knew he was carefully choosing his words and as the moments passed she found herself becoming impatient to hear them.

"You're too nice to be hurt, Kerry," he said at last in tones fringed with anxiety. "Will you mind if I'm outspoken?"

Although she flushed at this she was far too curious to bring the conversation to an abrupt end.

"Be as outspoken as you like, Charles." Her voice was pleasant but unemotional. Charles required careful handling. He desired to be more than a friend . . . yet he never struck Kerry as wanting to be in any way serious. She could be mistaken, of course, and his intentions could be entirely honourable. But as she had no feelings for him at all his intentions were unimportant, as Kerry had decided from the moment of his asking her to go out with him regularly.

"Perhaps you didn't know it yourself – but the way you looked at him on Wednesday, when you both stood there – well, that look was pretty revealing, Kerry."

Kerry started, genuinely surprised. She had scarcely spared Wayne a glance, she seemed to recall. And only about sixty seconds had elapsed before she excused herself and left the two men together.

"I – I don't know what you mean."

"I said that perhaps you didn't know it yourself." Reaching forward, he snapped off a sprig of jasmine from a bush close by and sat twirling it absently in his fingers for a moment before answering her question. "It so happens I've seen other women giving Wayne Harvey looks like that." Another uneasy pause and then, "Don't waste your time on him, Kerry –"

Kerry spoke before he could finish the sentence.

"I am not in love with the handsome, but wholly arrogant, insufferable and conceited Wayne Harvey!" The adjectives were meant to give strength to her denial, but Kerry realized the instant they were voiced that they must have quite the reverse effect upon her listener.

"So already you've been snubbed by him?" Whether or not the indelicacy of the question was intentional Kerry could not guess, but it certainly fanned her temper.

"It's time we put an end to this conversation," she said in quivering tones. "It's scarcely pleasant for either of us." Kerry stood up and Charles followed suit. Her eyes sought his face; she saw the compression of his lips and knew she had angered him.

"It certainly isn't very pleasant for me!" Charles turned abruptly and the movement brought him close to Kerry. "I know he has plenty that I haven't – but from your point of view it's rather profitless to flog a dead horse!"

Amazed, she stared at him.

"What a disgusting turn of phrase! If that's all you can conjure up in the way of conversational entertainment then please take me back to the hotel!"

"Don't be silly. We've come out to dinner."

"The prospect doesn't appeal any more. . . ." Kerry allowed her voice to drift away into silence, dismayed at her lack of diplomacy. She had known Charles required careful handling if she were to hold on to her job. In all probability she had lost it. And because she had been sending money to England she hadn't saved anywhere near enough for her fare back to England. What a muddle she was in – and all because of that legacy. To think, when making the bequest, her aunt would have been concluding that it would bring Kerry nothing but pleasure. Turning to her companion, Kerry spoke in low, troubled tones. "I suppose you're thinking of dispensing with my services?"

To her surprise and relief he immediately shook his head.

"No, Kerry. You happen to be efficient as well as beautiful. I can't afford to lose you – even though I know I'll never win you."

"Win?" Her eyes fell on the sprig of jasmine he still held between his fingers. Its perfume was heady even in small quantities and automatically she inhaled. "Your – your intentions were –"

"Of the most dishonourable, Kerry. Girls these days are cheap and men like bargains. I've always had double for my money where my receptionists were concerned."

Delicate colour suffused her face, but she kept a steady voice as she murmured,

"Always?"

A twinkle had entered his eyes; it broadened to a smile, and then he laughed and shrugged.

"There have been one or two who've held out."

"The last one, obviously."

"The last –? No – why should you say that?"

"She was engaged – at least, you said she'd left to get married."

A small pause and then,

"She wasn't engaged when she came to me." Explanation enough, but Kerry felt too disgusted to comment in any case. Must men always brag of their conquests? Why couldn't they be chivalrous and keep quiet about them? It was not difficult to imagine the conversation when several men got together. Kerry frowned, and swallowed convulsively. Would Wayne tell Charles that she, Kerry, had at the first attempt by Wayne given him some measure of reciprocation? More important, somehow, was the fear that Wayne might believe Kerry was another of Charles's "bargains", as he so crudely put it.

Charles was still smiling; the element of disunity had disappeared and Kerry returned his smile, giving an inward sigh of relief that her job was safe.

But during dinner Charles reintroduced the subject of Wayne Harvey. It seemed he just had to, and Kerry soon guessed that Charles was proffering another warning that Kerry's own chances with Wayne were nil.

"You met Rowena here that evening," Charles said unnecessarily, and Kerry had to smile to herself. Charles was still mildly piqued by Kerry's reticence over Wayne ... and he was still mildly jealous of Wayne. How relieved he would be were he to know just how deep went Wayne's contempt for her.

"Yes, I met Miss Blakely."

"She and Wayne are – well, more than friends, so it's rumoured." Kerry said nothing and Charles continued, again stressing the futility of any interest Kerry might have in Wayne, "If ever he did think of marriage, it would be to Rowena."

"You seem very sure of that."

"It's mere logic. No woman has held his interest for so long."

"He's had other women?" she asked curiously, and Charles's brows went up a fraction.

"A man like Wayne will always have women."

"Until he marries, of course – if ever he does marry, that is."

A faint smile that could only be described as a smirk touched Charles's lips.

"Does he strike you as a man who'll be faithful?" Charles shook his head and went on without waiting for a reply, "He's far too attractive. The world of women will always be at his feet. No, Wayne Harvey will never be faithful to one."

Just the conclusion to which she herself had come, thought Kerry, and a sudden frown knit her brow. Why this flat empty feeling all at once? Why should she care whether or not Wayne Harvey would remain faithful to one woman?

Throughout the evening she endeavoured to shake off the feeling of dejection, but it persisted and when at last Charles suggested they go home she breathed a sigh of relief. A night's sound sleep would prove effective in dispelling this despondency, the cause of which was ridiculous in the extreme.

But Kerry did not sleep soundly. On the contrary she tossed and turned for a considerable part of the night. For the dark and quiet hours encouraged a return of troublesome thoughts and memories. Wayne, thrusting her from his front door; Michelle, who had sighted freedom only to discover it was no more than a mirage. Avril, who dearly wished to see her younger sister. Irene – what news was it that could not be contained in a letter? Rowena and Wayne. . . . Suddenly Kerry felt his kisses again, insistent, demanding. Her own reciprocation . . . Wayne's arrogant expression of victory. . . .

The night wore on until at last, in the mists of approaching slumber all the people and incidents converged, and Kerry was desperately trying to disentangle them when at last she drifted into oblivion, mercifully rescued by sleep.

She was woken by slanting shafts of sunlight pouring through the shutters; she sat up, and frowned suddenly. Was it loss of rest which was responsible for this listlessness – this feeling of fatigue? It must be the result of depression, she decided, wondering if she would ever know peace of mind again.

For a moment, as she sat there staring at the furnishings of the room, Kerry almost wished she had never come into that legacy. Had she never seen it she would at this moment have been in the flat, humming a tune to herself as she prepared her breakfast. Then would follow a short but comfortable train journey, with the morning paper to scan on the way. The office and her very agreeable colleagues; lunch in the Silver Grill with several others from the office, a stroll round the shops before returning to her work. Kerry's evenings were in the main spent quietly, especially since Irene had begun going out with Stanley, but Kerry had regular dates with two friends, and she would sometimes spend the week-end with one or other of her parents. Yes, life had been unexciting but pleasant, and free from anxiety, whereas now.... Kerry wondered whether, had she her time to come over again, she would spend the money differently? She shook her head. No, she would still have spent it on finding her sisters. The only difference was that, having found them, she would then have acted less impulsively, both in Michelle's case and in Avril's. However, the damage was done now and all Kerry could hope was that Wayne Harvey would eventually come round and at least tolerate her. As for Michelle – she would have to continue as she was doing for the next few years, after which she would be free to live with Kerry if she wished.

The day seemed endless, as she sat at her desk, half expecting a call either from Avril or her uncle. And as the day wore on Kerry had an additional worry; she was becoming more and more lethargic with every hour that passed. Whatever was the matter with her? By the time Neville, the receptionist who was on duty throughout the night, came to relieve her, she felt almost ready to drop.

"Anything wrong, Kerry?" Neville examined her face anxiously. "You look very tired."

"I feel tired – utterly weary, in fact. I think I'll go straight to bed." A quivering hand was passed through her hair. Her brow felt clammy and the pain in her head was agonizing.

"I should," agreed Neville on an anxious note. "Do you think you ought to have a doctor?"

She managed a small laugh, shaking her head.

"Of course not. It's just tiredness; I'll be as right as rain in the morning."

But as she went upstairs Kerry wondered if she would be as right as rain in the morning, for she was as much affected by dampness of spirit as by her physical heaviness. Why hadn't Avril phoned? Had she been prevented from doing so by Wayne? He had not said a definite no when Kerry had asked if she and Avril could see one another, and somehow, despite his anger at being deceived, Kerry cherished the hope that he would unbend sufficiently to ring and give her his decision. But the day ended without her hearing either from Avril or Wayne, and when by six o'clock the following evening she had still received no communication Kerry felt more flat and depressed than ever. Physically, too, there was a deterioration, and on coming off duty she again decided to go to bed.

But on entering her room she sat there, staring into space. It was impossible to remain in this state of uncertainty and she began to toy with the idea of ringing up the Trade Winds Estate. Wayne had been much less hostile at the end of their encounter than at the beginning, she recalled, and with the passing of another half hour Kerry managed to gather sufficient courage to pick up the phone. Having learned from bitter experience the fatality of by-passing Wayne, she decided to ask for him and not for Avril.

Rowena Blakely's voice answered her. Kerry gave her name and asked to speak to Mr. Harvey.

"Mr. Harvey? What would you want with him? He's busy at the moment, anyway!" At the high-handedness of the reply Kerry's temper rose, a barrier to speech, and for a long moment there was silence on the line.

"I think," managed Kerry at last, although in rather choking accents, "that if you tell Mr. Harvey I wish to speak to him he'll come to the phone."

"Mr. Harvey has given instructions that he is not to be disturbed."

Kerry frowned. Was that true? It could be, she supposed, for with two large sugar plantations to manage most of Wayne's time would be taken up with important business matters. But surely he was not working at this hour, thought Kerry, automatically glancing at her watch. However, if Rowena refused to inform him that Kerry was on the phone there was nothing she could do about it.

"Avril ... is she there?" Hesitantly the question left Kerry's lips. Would Wayne be furious at Kerry's contacting Avril? Rowena did not answer immediately and when she did her tones were arrogantly crisp.

"What would you be wanting with Miss Harvey, might I ask?"

Something inside Kerry went tight.

"If my sister is there, Miss Blakely, then please bring her to the phone."

Another silence.

"Miss Harvey is out."

"Out?"

"That's what I said, Miss Fairclough."

Kerry bit her lip. Was Rowena telling the truth? There was no way of knowing and after a small hesitation Kerry said,

"Thank you, Miss Blakely." Replacing the receiver, Kerry entered the bathroom. But she had been there no more than two minutes when the phone rang and Neville told her there was a call for her. The next moment Kerry heard her sister's voice.

"Avril – I'm so glad you've rung! Have you tried to get me before?"

"Not yesterday, because Uncle Wayne wasn't sufficiently softened up."

Kerry blinked.

"Softened up?" she repeated rather breathlessly. And then she added before Avril could speak, "Where are you?"

"At home, of course."

"I've just rung and Miss Blakely told me you were out."

An angry exclamation from Avril, and then,

"She's hateful! I've been trying to ring you all afternoon, but she's always about and I somehow had the impression that if I picked up the phone she would listen in from Uncle Wayne's study, or even from her room. I don't know why I had that suspicion, but I did, so I waited. She's in the bath now and Uncle Wayne's in the garden – he's been there over an hour, relaxing for once, so I know I'm safe."

Kerry's eyes glinted. So Wayne was in the garden, relaxing, and not busy, as Rowena had asserted.

"Was your uncle very angry with you?" asked Kerry, putting Rowena Blakely out of her mind.

"Dreadfully," returned Avril, but in a tone that could only be described as light. "You, though – I expect he was absolutely furious. He told me he tackled you immediately I left the café. Was it very bad, Kerry?"

Bad? For some reason Kerry's memory skipped Wayne's fury and brought forward only the amorous demonstration to which he had subjected her in his office.

"I've managed to get over it," was Kerry's only comment.

"I was so anxious about you, but I knew he couldn't have actually hurt you in any way, so I didn't ring. You see, I hadn't finished working on Uncle Wayne. But let me begin at the beginning. He was like thunder when he tackled me, but I saw at once that his anger stemmed from my deceiving him and not because I'd been seeing you. This raised my hopes, but I went to work on him very cautiously. I cried and sobbed and was most contrite, but hinting in a subtle way that it was all his fault really. I said how would he like to have been kept from his brother – he and Daddy were very close, and I knew that would touch him. Well, Uncle Wayne is really very sweet and he loves me – that was my weapon, of course." A small laugh and then Avril added that it was a little difficult to retain her pose because with every passing moment her optimism grew. "He just couldn't bear to see me unhappy and he put his arms round me and comforted me. You know, Kerry, all men are basically the same, in that they possess the inherited traits of protection – I mean, it comes from cave-man days, doesn't it – when the male had to protect the female? And if a woman seems helpless and fragile, they fall like a ton of bricks. I kept it up all yesterday, saying I'd die if I didn't have you always, and at last he seemed ready to see reason – Oh, dear, he's getting up from his hammock," Avril digressed urgently. "He must be coming in. He and Rowena are going to a dinner party this evening. Now, listen, Kerry. As I've said, Uncle Wayne's awfully sweet, really, and so tender-hearted – Did you say something?"

"No," came Kerry's rather crisp response. "I merely gasped."

A tinkling laugh travelled over the line.

"You'll change your opinion of my uncle when you get to know him better."

"Shall I get to know him better?"

"That's the point of my ringing you. He's all softened up – I've done the spade-work. . . ." Avril's voice tailed off and there was silence for a moment. "Uncle Wayne isn't in the garden now. I wonder where he is? Never mind, he wouldn't listen in – at least, I don't think he would. To continue: ring him – as soon as I've put the receiver down, because in a few minutes he'll be going up to get ready for this silly old dinner party. I refused to go because they'll all be old fogeys and the men will sit there talking business. Ring Uncle Wayne, Kerry; put on a big act, pretending to be meek and humble. Apologize for encouraging me to deceit and don't forget to express anxiety about his treatment of me when he got home. Say it was all your fault and that you just had to ring and tell him so. Be terribly feminine and – sort of fragile and helpless. It'll work wonders – I've had proof, because I've done it before. Beg his forgiveness –"

"Beg!"

"Please, Kerry. It's awfully important. Ring – at once, while Rowena's out of the way. We talked for a long time today," Avril went on hurriedly, "and he's admitted you're my sister, but there seems to be something he doesn't like – and when I suggested such a thing he just refused to explain. But he'll soon learn how nice you are when he really gets to know you. . . ." A small pause. "I don't know where he is, Kerry," in a hushed tone now. "If he's gone to his office he could just pick up the phone. So I'll ring off, but you phone him at once – he's just in the right mood to see reason. I feel sure he'll make arrangements to see you and have a talk."

"Avril, I can't bring myself to be humble, and beg his forgiveness, as you want me to – Avril, are you there?" Silence. Biting her lip, Kerry stood for a moment and then replaced the receiver on its stand. Beg his forgiveness.... Never! After all he had done to her it was *he* who should beg *her* forgiveness.... She would not! "Definitely I won't! Crawl to a man like that – No, I definitely shall not!"

CHAPTER VII

Kerry paced the floor of her room. There was a line – and she had drawn it! Beg.... It was unthinkable. A couple of minutes elapsed. Avril would be waiting; Rowena was out of the way – but she wouldn't be for long. ... How could she have lied like that, saying Avril was out and Wayne busy? Serve her right if I did ring, thought Kerry, catching sight of her face in the mirror and wondering if it really belonged to her. Did she look as white as that? Still, it was understandable, considering the temper she was in. Beg! Rowena ... out of the way.

A further couple of minutes elapsed and then Kerry rang the Trade Winds Estate number.

"Trade Winds. Wayne Harvey here." Silence. It could have been the aftermath of temper that blocked her throat, but it wasn't. The simple explanation was that Kerry was tongue-tied. Why hadn't she thought of something to say before ringing the number? "Who's there?"

"It's – it's Kerry Fairclough...."

"Oh?" Kerry stared at the receiver. Was that hopeful? At least he hadn't rung off, as she half expected he would.

"Mr. Harvey . . . about Avril. Were you very – er – cross with her?" Kerry frowned in anger with herself. What had happened to her vocabulary?

"I expect Avril would consider that a rather mild word," came the smooth comment from Wayne, but it was quite sufficient to raise Kerry's hopes. Nevertheless it was with the greatest difficulty and drive that she managed at length to say,

"I rang to make an apology. I'm very sorry for encouraging Avril to deceit. I hope – hope you can overlook it – I mean –" She stopped. Beg? Impossible. "I really am very sorry," she ended lamely.

It was such a long while before Wayne replied that Kerry began to wonder if something had gone wrong with the line. But at last he spoke, and she almost dropped the receiver as she heard,

"If you care to come to my house, Miss Fairclough, we might have a talk."

"Yes, Mr. Harvey – er – when?"

"This evening. I'll expect you in about half an hour."

Half an hour? Avril had stated he would be getting ready for the dinner party. It would seem, then, that he wasn't going to give Kerry much of his time. It would be better to make arrangements for another day, Kerry decided, especially as she had never felt less like going out. During the last twenty-four hours there had been a gradual worsening of her physical condition; when she walked there was a strange weightiness about her thighs – as if they were too heavy. Consequently her legs felt weak, having to support too much weight, but it was the general feeling of debility that was beginning to worry Kerry. This was no mere tiredness, or even heat fatigue. The time had come when she was thinking of seeing a doctor.

"Mr. Harvey –" she began when she was interrupted.

"On second thoughts I'll send a car for you. It will be at the Beach Manor Hotel in about fifteen minutes' time." The receiver clicked and once again Kerry was left, wanting to say something, but unable to do so. Still, there was no doubting her keenness to get the matter straightened out and after a very quick shower in cold water and a brisk rub down she did feel a little better. Her spirits rose too, for it would seem that Avril was correct in her assumption that her uncle was ready to see reason.

Exactly half an hour later Kerry was being driven along the drive leading to the magnificent house standing on the rise. On reaching the wide pillared entrance the driver stopped the car and Kerry got out. The night was fragrant, dreamlike, with a disc six times its normal size spilling its shimmering phantom of moonlight over the house and grounds and trailing away in the indeterminate distance. From some equally indeterminate place closer to there drifted the compound heady fragrance of oleanders and roses, and of course the delectable jasmine. Silver pools of sea shone tantalizingly through gaps in the trees and other tropical vegetation. A perfect paradise of an island, thought Kerry, set as it was in the dancing Caribbean.

The chauffeur rang the bell; the door was opened almost immediately.

Cecilia smiled – a very different Cecilia from the half-scared dusky little girl who witnessed Kerry's previous humiliation.

"If you will come this way, missy?" Kerry followed her along the wide hall with its treasures and fabulous works of art and beautiful paintings, to a room beyond that to which Kerry had previously been shown. "I will tell Massa Harvey that you are here."

Reluctant to sit down without being asked, Kerry stood in the middle of the room, feeling that if Wayne didn't put in an appearance in the next minute or two she would certainly have to take possession of a chair. To her relief he did arrive, and she looked uneasily up at him, hoping to see a softened expression, but she was disappointed. His features were rigid and uncompromising; his flint-cold eyes regarded her a moment before he said, negligently flipping a hand in the direction of a chair,

"Take a seat, Miss Fairclough," which Kerry thankfully did, noting that Wayne was not yet dressed for dinner. There would be no time to talk, she thought, wishing fervently that she had had the chance to suggest another time for their meeting. Wayne's glance flickered to the door. "Cecilia!" he called, and the maid came at once, entering the room silently.

"Yes, Massa Harvey?"

"See that I'm not disturbed – not by anyone."

"Yes, I see to that, Massa Harvey."

Wayne took a seat and leant back, totally relaxed, adopting a far different pose from that of Kerry, who sat on the edge of her chair – even though she was fast reaching the point where she could gratefully have taken full possession of the most comfortable-looking couch.

"Now, Miss Fairclough," began Wayne in cool businesslike tones, "perhaps we can talk." She merely looked at him, and waited, and after a thoughtful moment he went on, "You'll be pleased to know that I now accept your relationship to my niece and am willing for you and her to visit one another." Cool and unemotional the voice; Kerry felt that only the self-confident Wayne Harvey could have made that admission without losing face. He would never lose face, she decided, sending him a glance from under her lashes and experiencing again that stirring of emotion. How easy it would be to fall in love with him. Many women must have done so, she thought, her mind straying automatically to Rowena Blakely.

"I can only say thank you, Mr. Harvey...." Kerry's voice faded out as listlessness overcame her. If only she could lie down! She must go back to the hotel, she suddenly decided, and half rose from her chair. "Mr. Harvey ... if you will excuse me. I'm afraid I can't stay to talk after all...." Kerry sank down again, looking apologetically at him.

"Is something wrong, Miss Fairclough?" he inquired, no interest whatsoever in his voice, but his face was a study of amused perception.

"I'm not very well...." What must she do? Kerry didn't even feel up to the ride in a taxi back to the Beach Manor Hotel. "I'm so sorry to – to be like this." To her astonishment Wayne merely yawned and leant back in his chair, making himself more comfortable and gazing at her with that expression of amused apprehension. Blankly she stared at him. Surely he had realized she was ill. Yes, he must have. Was he so utterly callous then, that he was going to carry on with what he meant to say, without even showing the slightest concern? Sweet and tender-hearted, Avril had said.... "Mr. Harvey ... would you call me a taxi?" Kerry put a trembling hand to her head, still looking blankly at Wayne, for he made no move to comply with her request.

"The act's quite unnecessary," he said in a faintly contemptuous voice. "The sooner you drop the helpless and – now what was it? Ah, yes – fragile pose the sooner we can get down to serious discussion. I want to know the entire history, for neither my brother nor his wife ever mentioned that Avril was one of a family of three – I said, drop the pose, Miss Fairclough!"

So he had overheard. How ironical that, with not the slightest intention of putting on the act suggested by her young sister, Kerry now felt so utterly ill and helpless that it must appear she was indeed acting a part.

He was waiting for her to say something, his eyes softer now, but only because of the mocking amusement in their depths. Feebly Kerry shook her head. An argument would only deprive her of what remaining strength she possessed, and she merely said,

"Mr. Harvey, if you don't get me that taxi I shan't be responsible for any inconvenience I might cause you."

At her words his eyes widened; he became alert and examining, and was instantly on his feet.

"You're not well?"

"I genuinely do feel off-colour." He stood close and she looked up at him, her face pallid and her lids drooping with tiredness. "I must go home."

Frowning, he stooped, drew the skin from under one eye and peered into it for a moment. Then his hand moved to her brow. His action was both unexpected and surprising, but by now Kerry had reached a point where she was too lethargic to feel anything but indifference.

"How long have you been feeling like this?" Wayne had removed his hand, but he still stood by her chair, watching her closely. "It hasn't only just come on." A statement, almost as if he knew what was wrong with her.

"No, it's been coming on for several days."

"Do you take plenty of salt in your food?" was his unexpected question, and Kerry shook her head blankly.

"Not much. I don't care for salt."

"You take salt tablets?" The very tone seemed to betray his conviction that she did not take salt tablets and again Kerry shook her head.

"No – why should I take salt tablets? I never have before."

Wayne drew an impatient breath.

"You perspire – not being used to our climate. Didn't it occur to you that you'd need to replace the salt you were so rapidly losing?" A disparaging quality to his voice and a flush rose to Kerry's cheeks.

"I didn't know about the salt tablets," she offered weakly, and again he gave an exasperated intake of his breath.

He strode over to the bell-rope and pulled it. Cecilia appeared as if by magic and Kerry had the impression that she had been guarding the door, obeying her master's command to the letter and making sure no one disturbed him.

"Yes, massa?"

"Fetch me the box of salt tablets and a glass of water."

"Yes, massa." With a swift glance in Kerry's direction Cecilia hurried from the room.

"It's been coming on for several days, you say?" He was by her chair again, quite overpowering in his tall magnificence. "I expect you've been feeling listless for much longer than that, but you haven't attached much importance to it. This is a slow thing and you don't notice it at first."

"I'm not really ill – just lacking in energy."

He was nodding thoughtfully even as she was speaking.

"You'll be all right in a day or two – but you must continue to take salt tablets while you're here. People who aren't used to our heat perspire heavily and in consequence lose the essential salt very quickly." He glanced up and a quick frown crossed his brow. "What is it, Rowena? I gave instructions I wasn't to be disturbed."

Rowena stood in the wide doorway, immaculate in a black cocktail dress. But her mouth was tight, and she stared at Kerry with a hostile light in her eyes.

"Cecilia said Miss Fairclough was here, and that she was ill. What's wrong?"

"Nothing serious. Cecilia's fetching some salt tablets."

Kerry glanced from Rowena to Wayne. His mouth was set and it struck Kerry that when he gave an order he expected it to be obeyed, no matter what the circumstances. Clearly he was annoyed with Rowena who, inevitably being familiar with his character, must have known she was risking his displeasure by the non-observance of his order. And this meant that Rowena's curiosity had risen above any fear she had of Wayne's anger. She just had to come in and see what was going on.

"Is there anything I can do?" The offer came reluctantly, as if Rowena had to say something.

"Nothing – oh, yes, ring Roger and make my apologies –"

"We're not going to the party?" Rowena spoke sharply, casting Kerry an almost malignant glance. "We can't disappoint him."

"There's nothing to stop you going," returned Wayne without much interest. "I'm certainly not going. Miss Fairclough here needs to be taken home – later, that is, when she's feeling better. I shan't have time to get ready."

"There's plenty of time for you to get ready. Miss Fairclough can go home in a taxi –"

"Ring Roger and make my apologies," cut in Wayne softly and, the colour mounting her face, Rowena withdrew rather hastily from the room.

Kerry looked up at Wayne.

"Mr. Harvey, there's no need to put yourself out. If you call a taxi I shall be perfectly all right."

"I'll take you back myself –" He stopped as Kerry, unable to hold up any longer, slumped against the back of the chair.

"I'm terribly sorry. . . ."

"You can't help it." His voice sounded rough, she thought, remembering Avril's assertion that the protective instinct was inherent in all men.

He looked up as Cecilia came in with a small box and a glass.

"Thank you, Cecilia."

"Will there be anything else, massa?" said Cecilia, with a brilliant flash of white teeth.

Wayne was taking the tablets from the box.

"Yes – I think you had better prepare a room for Miss Fairclough. She'll be staying the night."

"Yes, massa," replied Cecilia in an expressionless voice.

"There's really no need –" began Kerry when his glance cut her short.

"I think that by now you know me well enough not to argue." He handed her the tablets. "Take them, with a drink."

"Thank you." Kerry managed a wan smile and to her surprise it was returned. But instantly a frown appeared, this time because of the presence of his niece in the doorway.

"Oh, Uncle Wayne." Although Avril spoke to him she ran to Kerry. "Cecilia says you're not well! And – and you'll have to stay all night. Uncle Wayne, what's the matter with her? Is she very ill?" Tears stood on Avril's beautiful lashes; she appeared adorably feminine as she fluttered a glance at her uncle – feminine and fragile. Kerry looked at him swiftly. Yes, the shrewd light was in his eyes. Yet to Kerry's surprise it was almost instantly extinguished by the reflection of a smile.

"There's nothing seriously wrong with your sister, Avril. But she's certainly unfit to return to the Beach Manor tonight."

"Kerry. . . ." A faint sob touched Avril's voice despite her uncle's reassuring pronouncement. Kerry allowed herself a perceptive smile. The position between uncle and niece was both amusing and intriguing; Avril so sure she knew how to handle Wayne – and Wayne knowing exactly what she was up to but, apparently, treating her childish wiles with rather amused tolerance – yet he must know that Kerry would soon reveal to Avril that Wayne had listened in to her telephone call. "Do you feel terribly ill?" Without waiting for an answer Avril turned to her uncle. "If – if I l-lost her n-now. . . ." The sweet young voice faded away on a despairing frightened sob. Wayne regarded her with an expressionless gaze.

"That's a most unlikely eventuality," he assured her on a distinctly dry note. "If you want to make yourself useful go and find your sister some night wear and take it to the room Cecilia is preparing."

Miraculously Avril's tragic demeanour vanished.

"Yes, Uncle Wayne. Kerry shall have the very best I've got!" And she fairly danced from the room.

Wayne and Kerry exchanged glances; his voice retained its dry edge as he said,

"You've certainly made a hit with Avril. But then she doesn't know you were intending getting money out of her." Wayne's eyes never left Kerry's face as he spoke. Somehow she gained the impression that he would very much have liked her to deny that. But she was too vividly conscious of her blushes and air of guilt each time Wayne had suggested that she was here to get money from Avril, and although this time she did not blush, she couldn't with honesty deny her original intention.

"It was as I said," she told Wayne rather wearily. "The money was for my other sister."

"Michelle," said Wayne musingly. "Avril mentioned her."

Kerry glanced up, her heart beating much too quickly.

"You believe me, then – that I – we have another sister?"

Reaching out, Wayne took the glass from Kerry's rather unsteady hand.

"I don't know. I'll have your story just as soon as you're fit to talk." His keen observant gaze took in the hopeful light in Kerry's eyes, the quivering smile appearing on her lips. "Don't take anything for granted, Miss Fairclough. Whether you have another sister or not you'll never get your hands on a penny of Avril's money. My brother trusted me to take care of Avril and her money and that's exactly what I intend to do."

Kerry's smile faded; she looked down at her hands. The vision of release for Michelle died as quickly as it had appeared.

"The room's ready, massa," said Cecilia, standing at the door.

"Thank you, Cecilia." Wayne received a smile from the maid before she moved out of the doorway. "You can go at once," he said to Kerry. "There's no point in staying up. You'll feel much better when you're lying down."

"Yes." Kerry managed to stand, but walking proved quite a strain and when she was halfway across the room she stopped, shaking her head apologetically. "I don't know why I should be as bad as this —" Before she realized what was happening Kerry was lifted off her feet, with no more effort than if she had been a small child, and carried upstairs to the room assigned to her. Avril was there, laying a nightgown on the bed, a fabulous thing in peach nylon with three or four layers of ruched frills but scanty for all that.

Her big eyes opened very wide and she just stared in amazement on seeing Kerry in Wayne's arms. But she made no comment, merely dropping one eyebrow as Kerry glanced at her. So Avril also believed Kerry was acting a part.

Gently Kerry was put down in a sitting position on the bed.

"Don't worry," said Wayne on looking at her face.

"This will pass quite quickly. In a couple of days you'll be feeling fine."

"Is Kerry staying with us a couple of days?" Avril raised eager eyes to his; he smiled and nodded.

"I can't," exclaimed Kerry. "I have to be at work at nine in the morning."

"You won't be at work at nine tomorrow morning – or the following morning. I'll ring Charles and tell him where you are." Wayne turned to his niece. "Help your sister to undress, and then leave her –"

"Can't I sit with her, Uncle Wayne?"

"She'll be asleep five minutes after I've given her a drink."

Kerry said nothing, having reached a state of apathy towards everyone and everything around her. She didn't feel she required the drink Wayne intended giving her, but she refrained from saying so, feeling a protest would only be a waste of time.

When Wayne left, Avril did a little dance around the room, swirling and pirouetting with her dress held out.

"Aren't I clever! But you – oh, Kerry, you were superb! I didn't mean you to go that far – but I'm glad you did. Uncle Wayne carrying you upstairs – actually carrying you! If only Rowena had been there – She would have gone green – or even had a fit of some sort! I'm sure she would! And just imagine my uncle being taken in so easily!"

"Avril," said Kerry when at last she had the opportunity of speaking, "this is not an act, although your uncle did at first believe it was. You see, he overheard your call to me – or some of it at least –"

"Overheard? No!" Avril went a little pale. "Why didn't he say something to me, then? He can't have heard!"

"When I first said I was ill he was greatly amused, and

told me I could drop the pose as it was quite unnecessary. So obviously he had overheard."

"Oh dear. . . . ." Avril looked comical in her dismay and Kerry managed a rather feeble laugh. "So – so I wasn't really clever at all?" Avril frowned at her sister. "Why wasn't he angry with me?"

"I expect he had his reasons." A small thoughtful pause and then, "He seems amazingly tolerant with you, Avril. I think I can see what you mean when you say he's kind."

"You're already changing your opinion of him?" Avril didn't wait for an answer but said, anxiously scanning her sister's face, "Are you feeling very dreadful, Kerry?" The clouded look was very different from the triumphant expression which had greeted Kerry the moment Wayne made his departure from the bedroom. "Is it something serious?"

"Your uncle said it was nothing serious," Kerry gently reminded her. "You heard him telling me that I'd be all right in a day or two."

Avril helped Kerry to undress and then left her, as told to by Wayne.

Wayne entered the room ten minutes later and Kerry was given her drink.

"You're kind." She spoke on impulse; Wayne was standing by the bed, waiting for Kerry to drain the glass.

"Kind?" A quizzical smile appeared at the corners of his mouth and Kerry knew again that all-powerful emotion which was now becoming familiar. "That's the last thing I expected to hear from you."

Handing him the glass, Kerry leant back against the pillows. The situation in which she found herself was so unreal as to seem almost impossible. After all that had passed between Wayne and herself, the utter disgust and violence on his part, and the intense dislike on hers, here she was in his house, occupying one of his rooms, and also being looked after by him personally, for he could very well have sent Cecilia in with the drink, or Avril for that matter.

"You'll soon be asleep; and in the morning you'll feel much better." Striding over to the window, Wayne drew the curtains together, shutting out the moon-flushed splendour of the eastern sky. Returning to the bed, he stood looking down at Kerry's pale face for a long moment, an odd expression in his eyes. He seemed to be absorbing every detail, every lovely line and contour, every movement of her lips, every soft entrancing shadow cast by her long dark lashes. For her part Kerry lay there, looking upwards, trying to suppress the clamouring inquiry of her emotions while at the same time profoundly aware that this guardian of her sister's was, as she had already decided, possessed of a dangerous attraction. Dangerous? It could be fatal to some women . . . women who were foolish enough to fall in love with the man. Women bored him, Mick had said, but added that Wayne was also human, and presumably this was true, otherwise Rowena Blakely would not be occupying her present position, for she was certainly more than a mere secretary. For a moment Kerry dwelt on Wayne's treatment of her a few minutes ago. Curtly he had ordered her to ring his friend and make his excuses for not attending the dinner party. At one small protest from Rowena his manner had instantly become that of the employer, whose order this time had been obeyed without further argument.

With sleep gaining on her, aided no doubt by the draught given her by Wayne, Kerry could no longer keep her eyes open and as her lids dropped Wayne spoke, his voice soft and almost gentle.

"Good night, Kerry."

Kerry. . . . For the first time her name had left his lips. By that one word he had fully accepted her as one of the family. A rush of joy out of all proportion sped through her heart. It was reflected in the quivering smile and fleeting brightness of her eyes.

"Good night, Mr. Harvey – and thank you. . . ." She tailed off lamely; with a slight lift of his brows Wayne said,

"What for?"

She managed to hold her drooping lids in check for a moment as she gazed up at him.

"For being so kind."

"And . . .?"

Resignedly she said,

"For accepting me."

A long strange silence followed and then Wayne said softly,

"For accepting you. . . ."

Had Kerry been in full possession of her normally alert senses she might have wondered at his tone and manner. As it was she smiled up at him happily, fighting off the sleep which dragged at her consciousness.

"You won't forget to ring Charles?" she murmured as Wayne turned from the bed.

"No, I'll not forget." The sudden change of tone to one of stiff formality was startling and Kerry's heart seemed to twist with a tiny stabbing pain. Was he jumping to the wrong conclusions regarding her relationship with Charles? Twice Wayne had seen her out with him, she recalled.

"It's just so he'll know where I am," she murmured, in a tone gone suddenly flat.

"I'll see he knows at once where you are."

"What will you tell him? He doesn't know anything at all at present."

A slight hesitation and then, with a shrug,
"He'd better be told the truth."

"That I'm Avril's sister?"

"Yes, I don't see why not." And with that Wayne moved to the door, snapping off the light as he went out.

CHAPTER VIII

At nine o'clock the following morning Kerry's breakfast was brought up to her by Cecilia.

"Miss Avril want to come in, but Massa Harvey say no. He say to haf your breakfast and then haf some more rest. I fix anuder pillow so dat you can sit up."

"Thank you, Cecilia." Feeling much better, Kerry rather resented being made to stay in bed, but she had more sense than to disobey Wayne's order and on finishing her breakfast she put the tray on one side, removed the extra pillow and lay down again. Within ten minutes she was asleep; when she next opened her eyes it was half-past eleven and she wondered if it was her thirst that had wakened her. She rang the bell and Cecilia appeared. "Can I have a drink of water, please?"

"Yes, missy; I bring it now."

To Kerry's surprise the drink was brought in by Wayne along with her salt tablets.

"Had a good night?" Abrupt the tone, but edged with faint concern for all that.

"I slept wonderfully well, thank you." Kerry felt awkward, lying there in the great bed, with Wayne standing close, examining her face as if to assure himself that she had told him the truth.

"Sit up," he ordered and, unthinking, Kerry obeyed.

It was only on noticing his roving glance that she realized the scantiness of her attire. The top part of Avril's nightdress consisted of little more than two straps, daintily ruched and certainly decorative . . . but hardly adequate as a cover for Kerry's alluring feminine curves. Nor did Wayne spare her blushes as he continued to take his fill of her beauty. The flutter of her small hand, opening wide as it stole to her breast, served only to produce a hint of mocking amusement in her companion's eyes. "Take your tablets."

"Thank you." Kerry put them in her mouth before taking the glass from Wayne, so that she could keep her other hand where it was. After taking a long drink she handed the glass back and Wayne placed it on the table by the bed.

"Are you ready for that talk, or do you prefer to leave it until later?"

Profoundly conscious of her near-nakedness, Kerry shook her head, saying she would prefer to leave it until later, at which Wayne rose, picked up Avril's negligé from the back of a chair and handed it to Kerry; she thankfully draped it around herself, drawing the front edges together so that they met.

"Do you still want to leave it until later?" he queried, the gleam of amusement returning to his eyes.

A rather shaky little laugh escaped her.

"I feel more comfortable now. Yes, I'd very much like to talk, Mr. Harvey."

Nodding with satisfaction, Wayne brought up a chair and sat down. Reaching for the extra pillow, Kerry fixed it behind her shoulders.

"You'd better begin at the beginning," Wayne invited, and watched her face closely as she told her story. At the end he was frowning heavily. Remorseful? she wondered. This idea was strengthened when at last he spoke.

"So you spent the whole of your legacy on finding your two sisters?"

"All except the hundred pounds which brought me here." Her lovely eyes fixed his appealingly. "Mr. Harvey, I do realize now that I should have gone about things differently – what I mean is, I should have considered the possibility of Avril's not knowing she was adopted. You have no idea how upset I was when I realized what I'd done. It seemed that the money had brought nothing but misery to all of us."

Wayne was nodding his head in a preoccupied sort of way.

"I can only say you were badly advised by your solicitor," he commented after digesting Kerry's story. "Firstly, he should have anticipated the possibility of one or even both of your sisters being ignorant of their real parentage –"

"If it had been Michelle," put in Kerry, "it wouldn't have mattered. Mr. Haslett wrote to her parents and then visited them. Had they left Michelle in ignorance they would have told him and whatever their wishes on the matter I would have observed them, even if it meant my never meeting Michelle after all. But as everything was all right there, it never occurred to me that the same wouldn't be the case with my other sister."

"It didn't occur to you, no, because you were so enthusiastic about contacting Avril. But it certainly should have occurred to this fellow Haslett."

After a little thought Kerry nodded in agreement.

"Yes, I suppose it should." But then she added, "The fact that Avril was living abroad complicated matters."

"I don't agree. The businesslike procedure was for your solicitor, having ascertained that Avril had a guardian, to write to that guardian. A letter from a solicitor would have given a far different impression from that of the two you sent to my niece and which I kept from her in what, at the time, I believed to be her own interests."

Kerry gazed thoughtfully down at her hands. It was understandable that he should be suspicious, never having heard of the existence of Avril's two sisters.

"It's strange that your brother didn't tell you about Michelle and me," she said, looking up at him.

"I'm afraid my sister-in-law was extremely touchy about the fact that Avril was adopted. She couldn't have children of her own and this troubled her greatly." Wayne paused, preoccupied. It was as if he were considering just how much – or perhaps how little – he need say. That he intended saying more was evident and Kerry supposed he felt he owed her some explanation; in any case, he had said they'd have a talk, so obviously he intended making some contribution himself. And after a while he began to speak again and Kerry learned things her sister did not know. "I was away when my brother and his wife returned from England with Avril, for at that time my father was living and this was his estate. When I returned, to take over the management of Trade Winds – my father then being ill – I met Avril for the first time; she was then four and a half years old...." He stopped talking and Kerry looked swiftly at him, inquiringly. His mouth was strangely soft and she was reminded of Avril's assertion that her uncle was fond of children. "Your sister was very beautiful, even as a young child." Another pause; Kerry was surprised at Wayne's expansiveness, but thrilled and excited also that he should be speaking to her like this after his initial dislike of her. She leant back; her hair spilled in enchanting disorder over the pillow. The movement automatically brought Wayne from his preoccupation; he looked at her and his eyes flickered appreciatively. Then he smiled and her heart missed a beat as even yet again she silently declared him to be far too attractively masculine. "The first thing I noticed on my return was my sister-in-law's reticence concerning the adoption," Wayne continued at length. "I gained the impression that she was determined to forget altogether that Avril was not her own child. My brother did not talk either and I suppose he was respecting his wife's wish that the adoption should never be mentioned. As I've said, I was given no details whatsoever and, under these circumstances, I asked for none. I had no idea there were three of you and, thinking about this, I now realize there's a possibility that this information was in fact kept from my brother and his wife at the time of the adoption."

Kerry frowned and said,

"Surely such an oversight isn't possible?"

"It might not have been an oversight; it could have been intentional. I have no idea of the procedure attending an adoption, but I believe the minimum of information is given to the prospective parents."

"It's no wonder you suspected me," Kerry murmured understandingly. "Naturally you would jump to the conclusion that I was an impostor." Her eyes shadowed as she glanced at him. "With Michelle it was all so straightforward, and I naturally concluded it would be equally simple with Avril. Certainly I never envisaged these complications."

"The complication of a guardian, for instance?" Wayne's tone was dry.

"Mr. Harvey, I admit I intended asking Avril for money – when I learned how different her position was from that of Michelle – but my intentions were genuine in that I had no idea of any personal gain, unless of course it was that I'd have Michelle to live with me." No comment and Kerry persevered. "I admit I was impulsive in taking too much for granted. I was concerned about Michelle and naturally I believed Avril would also be concerned, and that she would be only too willing to – well, rescue her sister, as it were. I did explain to you that it was for Michelle," Kerry reminded him when he still made no observation on what she had said.

"It certainly did become a complicated situation," commented Wayne at last, "and for that I do blame your solicitor. It was his duty to write to me, explaining as fully as was necessary, and then I myself would have made the decision."

"Can I ask what decision you would have made, Mr. Harvey?" she asked curiously. Wayne was silent, engrossed in thought, and she added, "I rather think that you would have refused to have Avril disillusioned."

Wayne pursed his lips, and his brow creased in a frown.

"It would have been a most difficult decision, but I don't think it would have had the finality you suggest." He paused, because of the quick look of surprise she shot at him. "I most certainly would have insisted on a postponement, because it's little more than a year since her mother died."

"Some day, then, you would have considered telling her the truth?"

"I think I would, yes," he answered after a pause. "It would have been wrong of me to keep from her the knowledge that she had two sisters."

The admission was surprising, even though Wayne had now adopted a serious attitude towards her, unemotional, but by no means unfriendly.

"As I said once before to you, I would have abided by any decision you thought fit to make." This was an unintentional reference to the two letters which had been kept from her sister and for a moment Kerry held her breath, wishing she could re-phrase her words.

"As I've just said, had I received a letter from your solicitor it would most certainly have been treated very differently from those which you yourself sent. I suppose that as I'm businesslike myself I expect others to be the same. A letter from your solicitor would have been regarded as genuine, whereas those two letters from you were not." Kerry said nothing, and as the silent moments passed she wondered whether he were considering an apology. But he really had apologized – indirectly – and Kerry somehow knew that he would make no further reference to it. As she had told him, she now fully understood his suspicions; it was unbusinesslike for her to write directly to some unknown girl, saying she was her sister.

"Perhaps Mr. Haslett didn't write to you because the money had run out," she suggested as the thought suddenly occurred to her. But Wayne shook his head.

"You had a hundred pounds left," he reminded her. "No, it was simply an oversight on the part of this Mr. Haslett – and an oversight which has caused a great deal of unnecessary trouble."

"Rather more than trouble," was Kerry's impulsive rejoinder, and a smile once again softened the hard line of Wayne's mouth.

"Your stay on Barbados has been rather unpleasantly eventful," he remarked, and Kerry wondered if he were remembering, among other incidents, that one in his office. At the recollection she lowered her head, and began fingering the lovely hand-made lace with which Avril's negligé was trimmed. It was an intensely nervous movement watched by her companion through narrowed eyes, and presently she was unable to resist an upward glance from under her lashes and she noted his interest in her every small movement, keen and perceptive. She forced herself to keep her hands still. The atmosphere was tense, alive, and for one wildly frightened moment she visualized him taking her in his arms again. From that last encounter she had emerged thankfully convinced that she would never again be subjected to the kind of temptation which only a man so superlatively male as Wayne Harvey could exert, yet here she was, in an equally dangerous – and undoubtedly more vulnerable – position than before. Involuntarily Wayne hitched his chair forward and she jumped.

"What's troubling you, Kerry?" he inquired in some amusement.

"Troubling m-me?"

"Whom are you afraid of – me, or yourself?"

"Is that the question a gentleman would ask?" she retorted unhesitatingly, and to her amazement Wayne's expression took on a quality of mock disappointment.

"I've been cheated," he said, by-passing her question. "I expected to throw you into enchanting confusion."

She stared bewilderedly at him.

"You're a strange man," she murmured, almost as if she were speaking her thoughts aloud.

"Incomprehensible, you mean?"

He might well say that, Kerry thought, recalling how many varying facets to his nature she had already seen.

"Yes; I don't understand you at all."

"Strangely, nor do I understand you, for you never react to a situation in the way you should." Frowning, Kerry asked him what he meant.

"Well, as you were genuine, your natural reaction when I sent you from my house should have been to write to me and give a long and full explanation."

"When you sent me from your house? When you threw me out, you mean," Kerry couldn't help saying. "I landed in a bed of prickly pears – or something like that," she added irrelevantly, and a half frowning, half laughing expression lit Wayne's eyes.

"You did?" No comment from Kerry and he added, in a strangely gentle tone, "Do you expect an apology?"

"Would I receive one if I did?" she swiftly challenged, and he slowly shook his head. "Then, unlike me, you do react in the way I expect you to."

"A nasty riposte," he laughed. "You haven't much of an opinion of me." A statement, and not expecting any comment he went on to ask again why she hadn't immediately written him a letter.

"I was too occupied with my financial position, wondering how I was to get back to England. Then, very soon, Mick – that's the young man who did the investigating," she added, but Wayne was already nodding his head and Kerry went on to explain how he had found her the post at the Beach Manor Hotel.

"I see. . . ." He paused meditatively. "And now of course you can't return, not immediately, because you've committed yourself to sending money to Michelle's parents?" She merely nodded and he changed the subject. Referring to another occasion when her reaction had been different from what he would have expected, he asked baldly why she hadn't slapped his face that day in his office when he kissed her. Naturally this brought the colour rushing to her cheeks and she swiftly averted her head.

"I suppose I should have," said Kerry unevenly, her voice rising little above a whisper. Wayne's glance was quizzical.

"I suggested you liked it," he reminded her with brutal lack of consideration for her feelings, and she sent him a speaking glance. His eyes were still laughing at her and Kerry's colour heightened still further. But she made no comment and he repeated, with that hint of satirical mockery she had previously encountered, "No, Kerry, you never react in the way one would expect."

With a quick kindling of anger she retorted, looking challengingly at him,

"Perhaps one day I might – and it's to be hoped you won't be disappointed!"

Wayne's lids came down, in a sort of lazy way; her half-threat troubled him not at all!

"We appear to have digressed," he remarked at last. "Getting back to this business of you and Avril. What exactly have you in mind regarding the future?"

"I've no definite plan – not now. Things will have to continue as they are for the present." She became lost in unhappy brooding as she recalled her first eager plans for an exciting reunion with both her sisters. Then her thoughts switched to that passage in Irene's letter, the passage saying she had something to tell Kerry about Michelle. But there was nothing to be gained by worrying about that until she knew what it was. "You'll let Avril and me see each other regularly?" she asked, quite un-aware of her appeal as her lovely eyes met his. Nor did she catch the sudden intake of his breath.

"I've no objection to that." A small reflective silence and then, "Tell me, how much were you expecting to get from Avril?"

It was some time before Kerry answered. But why hesitate? It was clear that Wayne meant to have an answer, and resignedly she said,

"Three thousand pounds –"

"Three thousand!"

Kerry swallowed, turning a flawless profile towards him.

"It didn't seem much – seeing that Avril was so wealthy. I can't expect you to understand, though, because you haven't seen Michelle." Fully expecting that to be countered by some caustic remark about its making not the slightest difference if he did see Michelle, Kerry was astonished to hear Wayne say thoughtfully,

"Three thousand. . . ." And then he looked at her so

strangely that a sudden access of misgiving invaded the depth of her senses. Had the idea not been ridiculous she could have suspected Wayne of some intended mischief! "Three thousand," he repeated, and this time her apprehension grew out of all proportion.

"It doesn't matter," she said hastily, although she couldn't have given a reason for this, because of course it was important, especially if Wayne were actually considering allowing Avril to advance the money.

Ignoring her words, Wayne said,

"This business – it's still for sale?"

"Yes." Why no enthusiasm on her part? Why no excited fluttering of her heart? Then Kerry realized her heart *was* fluttering . . . but not with pleasurable anticipation. What was the cause of this perilous feeling? "It doesn't matter," she said again in unmistakably urgent tones. "I'll – I'll just carry on l-like this."

His eyes sharpened. Somehow, Kerry had the impression that her declaration did not suit him at all.

"You no longer want your sister to be taken out of that unsuitable environment?"

He was tying her in knots; she couldn't honestly say no – but for some odd reason she was disinclined to say yes.

"Things are different from what I expected," she said evasively at last, and to her relief Wayne probed no further, but instead he asked curiously,

"Have you mentioned anything to Avril about this three thousand pounds?"

"No, of course not."

"I thought you hadn't –" A small significant silence and then, with emphasis, "Don't, Kerry, understand?"

She nodded her head.

"Yes, I understand."

"You look tired," Wayne observed, rising and replacing

the chair in its original position by the wall. "Have another sleep and you might be able to get up for dinner."

"Can't Avril come in?" Kerry asked as Wayne was leaving the room, and after a small hesitation he nodded.

"For a few minutes," he said, "but that's all. You need sleep."

"I must stay only ten minutes," Avril was saying with a grimace a few minutes later as she sat on a chair drawn up beside her sister's bed. "Uncle Wayne has already told me that everything's all right, and that I can ask you here just whenever I want, but you tell me some more – everything he said, in fact!"

Smiling a little ruefully, Kerry told Avril as much as was necessary – and there was certainly a good deal to be left out!

"I knew he was ripe for surrender," Avril commented in a self-satisfied way when Kerry had finished her narrative. And with a swift sideways glance at Kerry she added, "Have you changed your opinion of him now, as I prophesied you would?"

"Partly," was all the concession Kerry would make, for she was again experiencing that odd tremor of danger – of indefinable, and seemingly absurd apprehension about something nameless and intangible.

"Don't you find him devastatingly handsome?"

Kerry smiled. There was no doubt that Avril adored her guardian.

"Yes, I admit he's handsome."

"He's really sweet, too, when you get to know him, of course. I've known him ever since I can remember. He was always good for a jolly game, and he used to toss me up high and catch me, and it was Uncle Wayne who taught me to swim and play tennis and dance. I love him very much and it was awful when it appeared that you and he weren't going to be friends." Glancing at her watch as she spoke, Avril frowned. "My ten minutes are almost up, and if I'm not downstairs soon Uncle Wayne will be cross. It's no use arguing with him, either; I know how to handle him, but I also know when to give in. Uncle Wayne does like to be the boss – for most of the time."

"But not all the time?" and when Avril gave a negative gesture, "You surprise me." Kerry's tones were dry and Avril laughed, tossing her head so that the golden hair sprang from her face, then fell again, caressing her cheeks.

"You made a bad impression."

Kerry agreed, then said,

"I expect your uncle tackled you about that telephone call? He knew you'd advised me to put on an act."

Another grimace, but Avril was not in any way put out.

"He told me off, and said I was a wretch. I retaliated by saying he had no right to be listening in to my call. Wasn't it a priceless situation! Your being genuinely ill just at that time, and Uncle Wayne naturally taking it for granted that you were putting on an act –" Avril broke off, half-apologetic, yet there was laughter in her eyes for all that. "I didn't want you to be ill, of course."

"But you're thinking it was most opportune, nevertheless," supplemented Kerry, her own face alight with amusement.

"It seems to have done the trick more speedily than anything else could." Avril looked at Kerry, and shook her head in a gesture of disbelief. "That he would actually carry you upstairs! I do wish Rowena had happened to see it all."

"Why don't you like Rowena?"

"She's too high-handed – but I don't think it's that."

"No? What is it, then?"

"I'm possessive, I suppose," Avril admitted after a re- flective pause. "I'd dislike anyone who stood a chance of becoming Uncle Wayne's wife."

"Has Rowena a chance of becoming his wife?"

"I never can decide," admitted Avril after some thought. "I believe they're having an affair – and Uncle Wayne does take her out quite a lot. But somehow I don't think he'll marry Rowena – for two reasons. Firstly, he's just the man to despise her sort secretly, if you know what I mean? And secondly, she's hard and arrogant, and I always imagine Uncle Wayne with someone soft and pliable and terribly, terribly in love with him."

Kerry thought about this. How fatal to be terribly, terribly in love with a man like Wayne. One would have to be more than pliable, one would have to become subordinate to his every wish and desire, to submerge one's own identity in his, almost.

"Rowena," she said as if forced to mention Wayne's secretary again. "Does she – I mean, is she of the opinion that Wayne will eventually marry her?"

"Oh, I think so. Just lately she's become more high-handed than ever, just as if she was practising for when she takes over as mistress of Trade Winds."

A sudden little ache gripped Kerry's throat ... and something clamoured for admission, something which Kerry thrust away with a haste akin to panic.

Abruptly she changed the subject, asking Avril if her uncle had said anything about Michelle.

"No – but the next thing is to persuade him to give me some money so that I can have Michelle over for a holiday."

Kerry thought about this. She was sure that Michelle's father, disappointed as he was at not getting the three thousand for the business, would say a definite no to any request that Michelle should have a holiday with her sisters. Also, it had recently occurred to Kerry that it might not be a good thing for Michelle to come to Barbados, after all. Should she come, she would have a fleeting glimpse of paradise, then return to her drab environment carrying the picture of Avril in all her luxurious and exotic surroundings; and Michelle being so young, she must surely feel envious of her sister. Previously, with her mind occupied only with the rosy prospect of a reunion, Kerry had not considered this aspect of the situation, but now she was coming to the conclusion that it might be cruel, rather than kind, to bring Michelle to Barbados – even should her father allow it.

"I shouldn't ask your uncle yet," she advised, and Avril nodded in agreement.

"We must proceed slowly." A small silence and then Avril said, her voice fringed with anxiety, "You never say much about Michelle – oh, you've told me what she looks like and the kind of home she lives in, and said a little about her parents and brothers and sisters, but –" Avril broke off, frowning to herself. "Is everything all right with Michelle?"

Believing she had successfully kept the true position from Avril, Kerry was naturally startled by her sister's question.

"How do you mean, all right?" she parried.

"She's happy?"

"She hasn't been as fortunate even as I," Kerry replied after a long uncertain silence. "Her parents are quite poor."

"I gathered that from what you've told me." Avril's voice held a tinge of impatience. "I mean, is she happy with her adoptive parents?"

Another silence. Wayne would not be pleased if Avril became troubled about Michelle's situation, Kerry knew. Yet how was she to answer Avril's question?

"I must admit I've thought a lot about Michelle," Avril went on as the silence continued. "And that's because you always seem to evade a long discussion about her. It would hurt me if she wasn't happy – being so young. After all, she's only a little girl, and if she were unhappy as well as being poor –" Avril broke off as the door opened; with a heartfelt sigh of relief Kerry saw Wayne standing there, immaculate in a suit of white linen, his face set and stern.

"Avril, have you forgotten what I said?"

"I'm sorry, Uncle Wayne. I – I was just going."

His eyes narrowed.

"I gave you ten minutes – and that is ten minutes ago."

"I'm sorry," said Avril again, lowering her head. Wayne turned to Kerry.

"I thought you'd like to know that your absence from work is not causing too much inconvenience to Charles. He's just rung to ask how you are, and at the same time to say that the girl who left him to get married came into the hotel with her husband last night, and when she knew Charles was temporarily without a receptionist she offered to come in for a week –"

"A week!" exclaimed Kerry and Avril together, but with very different expressions on their faces.

"I couldn't stay off work a week –"

"Is Kerry staying with us for a whole week?" interrupted Avril excitedly.

"But, Mr. Harvey, I can't!" Kerry stopped. Wayne was now looking down at Avril in the sort of way that made Kerry gasp. That he was capable of love was more than clearly evident ... if only the kind of love an uncle feels for his niece.

"Is that what you want, dear?" he asked, and it would seem that Kerry's protests had completely passed him by.

For an answer Avril tucked her arm into his, looking up at him with a mingling of gratitude and happiness in her eyes.

"You're the best uncle in the world," she whispered huskily.

"And on that note of flattery we'll leave your sister to take her rest." Wayne's eyes moved from Avril's animated little face to that of Kerry, who had opened her mouth to make a further protest, and then closed it again. "You'll not feel like getting up for dinner if you don't sleep," he warned, removing Avril's arm and walking to the door.

A few minutes later Kerry was lying down, relaxed in body but confused in mind. A whole week here with Avril ... and Wayne.... She really should have voiced stronger protest, for something warned her she was courting disaster.

CHAPTER IX

BIRD song and perfume ... soft heady air ; the murmuring breeze in the palms and the tang of the sea ; the wild flaring sunset....

Sitting alone on Wayne's private beach, her scantily-clad golden body contrasting with the silver sand, Kerry felt almost drugged by the sheer beauty of the coral island scene. The sun was dropping slowly towards the horizon, but its rays were still hot and Kerry leant back on her elbows, a contented sigh issuing from her lips. It was four days since the evening of her visit to the Trade Winds Estate, and since her subsequent indisposition which, to all appearances, had been instrumental in resolving the difficulties which had hitherto existed between Wayne and herself. It had been a lazy, idyllic time of swimming in the warm tropical sea, of sunbathing in the uncrowded comfort of Wayne's private beach, of delicious meals and carefree conversation with Avril and her uncle. Avril had taken her to see her own house – a Regency mansion rather similar to Wayne's in that it had the same elegance and space inside and the same type of verandahs, ornamented by fluted columns made of soft, ochre-coloured coral. Its gardens were full of cups of gold, poinsettias, and of course masses of bougainvillea and hibiscus. Mangoes and paw-paw trees mingled with breadfruits and palms, while stretching as far as the eye could see was the plantation itself, with the labourers working among the sugar canes. Kerry's happiness was due to the fact of her being with her sister, she constantly told herself, but there was no doubt that Wayne's changed attitude towards her had a great deal to do with her new-found peace of mind. Always friendly and charming, he smiled at Kerry often, laughed at her now and then, and it did seem that he was disproportionately eager to establish a harmonious relationship with her. For her part Kerry responded, often aware of her heart's excited rhythm – but just now and then disturbed when that rhythm gave way to a tumult of apprehension on the wake of which would come a recollection of that access of danger experienced on the occasion of her acquiescence over the matter of her remaining at the Trade Winds Estate for a whole week.

Rowena missed nothing and as Wayne's friendliness towards Kerry grew, so did Rowena's hostility, and whenever she found herself alone with Kerry she would adopt a condescending manner which would bring Kerry up with a jerk, reminding her that Rowena was Wayne's girl-friend, and that it was natural she should resent the attention now given by Wayne to Kerry.

However, as yet Kerry had been caused no real discomfort by Wayne's secretary, mainly because she and Rowena had rarely been alone, Rowena being away at the office during most of the day. Kerry was alone this afternoon simply because Avril had an appointment at her hairdresser's in Bridgetown. She should be back directly and would most probably join Kerry on the beach.

Dismissing Rowena from her mind, Kerry began to muse reflectively on the short conversation she'd had with Charles the day before yesterday when, driven by Wayne's Negro chauffeur, she had gone to the Beach Manor Hotel to fetch some of her clothes and other necessities. Charles had expressed his indignation that she had not been open with him when he had asked the reason for Wayne's interest in her.

"Why the secrecy?" he had added, studying her face as if expecting to find some difference in it. "There was no reason for it that I could see."

"I didn't know if Wayne – Mr. Harvey would want you to know I was Avril's sister."

"For heaven's sake, why?"

Kerry gave a slight intake of her breath.

"It was my own private affair, Charles," she replied, remembering how Wayne had presumed that she couldn't keep her business to herself. "After all, I'm only an employee here, so there was no reason why I should tell you about my relationship to Wayne's niece."

Charles shrugged.

"So it's Wayne now, is it?" he digressed, looking closely at her.

"That's not surprising, seeing that he's my sister's uncle."

"In that case," said Charles with a faintly sardonic tone, "you should also be calling him uncle. In fact," he added, "it's a wonder he didn't insist upon your doing so."

As Kerry made no comment on that Charles lost interest and Kerry went up to her room to collect what she required. When she came down Charles was engaged in conversation with one of the guests and merely said,

"I'll see you on Monday, then?"

Kerry nodded.

"Yes – and thank you for letting me have the time off."

"Don't trouble to thank me," was the rather dry rejoinder. "One learns not to go against the wishes of a man like Wayne Harvey."

A movement in the near distance interrupting her thought stream, Kerry brought her dreamy gaze from the undulating sea and looked towards the house. Visible through the trees at the bottom of Wayne's garden was a tall bronzed figure, clad only in trunks.

Wayne stopped on reaching her and looked down – seeing everything, she thought, frowning slightly as she realized he always regarded her like this, just as if her body were of immense interest to him. Colour tinted her cheeks; a quirk of amusement touched the corners of Wayne's mouth as he sat down on the towel she had spread out to dry on the sand.

"You're very beautiful, Kerry," he told her softly, his lips close to her ear. "I believed until recently that I'd never meet a more beautiful girl than your sister."

Kerry did not know what to say. She had been flattered before, naturally, but never by anyone like Wayne, and she felt gauche, tongue-tied in a way she would never have believed possible.

"I don't think I'm prettier than Avril," she murmured awkwardly, and then wished she hadn't, because of the slight mocking lift of Wayne's eyebrow.

"Very feminine," he commented, his gaze roving again. But his eyes smiled and Kerry managed a difficult smile in response. Shyly she looked at him, noting the mahogany of his skin, the deep forest of hair on his chest and forearms, the muscles on his shoulders. She swallowed something hard in her throat, so profoundly affected by him that she turned away, lest he should make a

147

guess at her feelings. Her feelings . . .? What were they? With a sort of combative desperation she endeavoured to avoid the answer . . . but it came – like a deluge in which she floundered, helplessly.

"I'm not in love with him," she tried to tell herself. "I'm not!"

"Have you been in the sea?" Idly Wayne picked up a shell, a lovely peach and pearl creation, and held it in his hand, admiring its superlative beauty.

"Yes – twice." Was this her voice? It sounded cracked and husky, but to her relief Wayne did not notice.

"Feel like another dip?"

Kerry hesitated. Far safer to be in the sea than to sit here, talking.

"Yes, I'd like to go in again." But then she added, "Avril – is she not back yet?"

Wayne looked quizzically at her.

"Do we need a chaperone?" he inquired disconcertingly.

"Of c-course not."

Rising, he held out a hand.

"Come on, then." His fingers curled round hers as they walked to the edge of the sea. The gesture sent tremors running through her. He released her only when they had waded out far enough for them to swim. Was her position so hopeless after all? Supposing – by some miracle – he liked her? Liked her in that sort of way? The idea left her breathless, and she made no effort to swim beside Wayne, but she watched him dreamily as she lay on her back, floating in the crimson sunlight. Swinging around, he came back; he teased her, calling her lazy, and she laughed. Whatever the outcome this was an exquisite moment and she forgot everything else as she gave herself up to the full enjoyment of it.

"I feel lazy," she retorted, because in her shyness she

couldn't think of anything else to say.

"Then come on out and be lazy on the beach." The tone was vibrant; Kerry thrilled to it and followed as he swam towards the shore. He took her hand again as they made for the spot where the towel lay. Stooping, Wayne caught up the towel and gathered Kerry's hair into it; startled by his unexpected action, she stared up at him, her cheeks flushed beneath their newly-acquired tan, her lips parted as if pleading for a kiss. Wayne's eyes took on the darkness of desire; his hands became idle and Kerry felt the towel slide down her wet back as it dropped on to the sand. This was madness, she knew, but she was powerless to resist as she felt herself being drawn into a gentle embrace and felt Wayne's cool clean breath on her face before his lips closed on hers. Above, the burnished, cloud-scattered sky lent its brilliance to the sea and sand, and draped the tree-tops in a scarlet veil of lace. Overwhelmed both by the exotic setting and the power and magnetism of the man in whose embrace she was held, Kerry became lost in the magic of her own desire.

"Kerry. . . ." Wayne held her from him at last, his eyes soft now, soft and gentle as his kisses. A trembling little sigh escaped through lips warm and rosy from his tenderness. "What have you done to me?"

Unbelievable words! – surely a declaration of love. Deep and profound her emotions as in wordless ecstasy she pressed against him, her small hands caressing his shoulders. His lips sought hers again, demanding, possessive. And a long time elapsed as they stood there, the sole occupants of the beach, lost in a spell of ardour and sweetness, of fanned desire and determined restraint. Temporarily released again, Kerry shone up at him, shaking her lovely head as if to ward off the increasing pressure of the spell.

"What is it?" His eyes were smiling and tender, hers

shyly becoming hidden by long curling lashes that threw adorable shadows on to her cheeks. "God, but you're beautiful!" His lips were on her hair, then her neck; they wandered down to her shoulder and still further to the uncovered curve that beckoned and tempted, inviting further exploration. Kerry's pulse raced in sympathy with the sudden spinning of her mind; it was as if the world had stopped rotating and she was being hurled into the intoxicating lightness of space. But by some forced exertion of will she managed to insert a hand between his lips and their object. And he didn't immediately remove her hand, as he could so easily have done, but merely lifted his head and looked down at her quizzically. Relief brought a flutter to her lips that was hardly a smile, but her eyes now unashamedly revealed her love and Wayne's laugh of tender triumph broke on to the bewitching silence around them.

"We must go back...." His voice became an indistinct murmur against her cheek as he kissed it. "The breeze is blowing cool – and in any case dusk is on us." He stooped for the towel and draped it round her, tilting her face so that he could take his fill of the revelation of her eyes.

Although Kerry now had most of her clothes with her, she possessed nothing which could be remotely described as glamorous, and as she wanted to appear especially attractive that evening at dinner, she took advantage of Avril's previous offer of a free run of her wardrobe, choosing an expensive creation of lime-green, with a tight-fitting bodice and low-cut neckline. With its full but short skirt it did just about everything for Kerry, being both flattering to her figure and colouring and also to her shapely slender limbs. Her hair, which she had hastily washed after its several sea-drenchings, shone like burnished bronze as she brushed it, and with a little access of excitement she actually saw Wayne's appreciative eyes wandering slowly over her.

She was just taking a last look in the mirror when Avril knocked on the door and asked if she could come in.

"Of course." Kerry turned from the mirror as the door opened.

"Kerry!" Avril stood stock still, gazing in rapt admiration at her sister. "You look ravishing! What have you done to yourself?"

Automatically Kerry twisted round to take a look in the mirror. Was this what love did to you? – sprinkled your eyes with starlight and brushed enchanting colour over your cheeks?

"Your dress," she said briefly, but Avril was shaking her head.

"You look as if you've come into a fortune."

"It's simply that I'm happy," she laughed.

Avril came further into the room and smiled affectionately at her.

"Because of me – or Uncle Wayne?"

"Uncle Wayne?" sharply. Surely Avril hadn't guessed?

"Because he's no longer mad at you."

Kerry breathed again.

"Yes, that's part of it," was all she said, naturally.

"Part?"

"You're the other part, of course. It's been wonderful staying here with you."

"It's been wonderful for me too. And we've three more days left yet, and even after that we'll see each other often."

"Certainly we shall." Kerry spoke with confidence, her thoughts flying to Wayne and the sweet new relationship which had begun between them. Surely it would grow and strengthen ... and then. ...

When she and Avril came downstairs Wayne and Rowena were on the terrace, engaged in conversation. Wayne rose at once and brought forward two chairs.

"More beautiful than ever," he whispered from behind her head as she sat down, and a sudden all-pervading warmth reflected itself in the rosy mantling of her cheeks. Her eyes strayed to Rowena, drawn there forcibly. The girl's eyes were narrowed in an expression of deep animosity. Her jealousy was patently clear and a twinge of guilt rose to mar the pleasure Kerry had derived from Wayne's low-toned words of flattery. Rowena was Wayne's girl-friend; in Avril's opinion she hoped to marry him some day. It suddenly seemed wrong for Wayne to kiss another girl, especially in the way he had kissed Kerry only a short while ago. Those other kisses meant nothing; they were forced on Kerry in order to teach her a lesson, but down there on the beach Wayne's kisses had portrayed all the tenderness of love.

Avril was chattering away in her gay tones and Wayne was smiling indulgently as he listened. Avril asked him if he liked her hair-do and he said yes, at which she then chided him because he hadn't noticed she'd had it styled differently today.

"Not very differently," he said, examining it now with interest. "You've not had it cut or anything drastic like that."

Avril kept up a flow of chatter, but Kerry turned her attention to the large Negro who was making some special kind of drink.

"Punch," elucidated Wayne on seeing her expression.

"It's lovely. Only Medvil can make it properly." Avril smiled at Medvil, who showed his appreciation of her flattery by flashing her a broad smile which revealed two rows of fine white teeth. Medvil dropped the peeled limes into the bowl, then lemon peel and nutmeg. Sugar and water followed and finally white rum. After the brisk use of the swizzle-stick the punch was ready to drink.

"Like it?" Avril watched Kerry as she sipped from her glass.

"Yes . . . I think so."

"You don't seem very sure, Miss Fairclough." Rowena spoke in a sarcastic, condescending tone which couldn't possibly go unnoticed by the others, and both Wayne and Avril turned to look at her. Wayne's eyes flickered to Kerry, who managed a laugh as she suggested that punch might be an acquired taste. No one spoke, but presently the moment was eased by the appearance of Cecilia announcing that dinner was ready.

The island's natural foods were very much in evidence; Kerry had her first taste of the delicious sea-eggs, fried in butter, and instead of potatoes she was served *beignets* of breadfruit, which was rather like potato, but lighter and far more appetizing.

Dinner over, they all retired to the verandah as usual. But it was getting late and after chatting with the others for about half an hour Kerry asked to be excused, saying she was going to bed.

"So soon?" Wayne added a frown to the question; Kerry noted the swift change of Rowena's expression as the smile she was flashing at Wayne instantly faded.

"It's quite late," Kerry reminded him, husky-voiced. Did he want her to stay? It would seem like it, she decided with a sudden spread of pleasure.

"I think I'll go too." Avril rose from her wicker chair and kissed her uncle. Her "Good night" embracing both Wayne and Rowena, she turned to Kerry. "Coming?"

Kerry nodded, glancing at Wayne. There was an instant of hesitation and then he shrugged.

"Good night." His glance was directed first at Kerry and then at Avril.

There was now no way to avoid leaving and, feeling a little flat all at once, Kerry bade Wayne and Rowena good night in low-toned accents and followed her sister into the house.

"I didn't know whether to be spiteful and stay," said Avril as soon as they were out of earshot. "But then I thought: let them get on with it."

"Get on with what?"

"Making love – I expect that's what they do when they're alone."

An unusual dryness clawed at Kerry's throat. Yet instantly her mind leapt to that scene on the beach and Wayne's tender words, "What have you done to me?"

"I – I don't believe your uncle's in love with Rowena." They were ascending the stairs to the balustraded gallery off which the bedrooms opened. Kerry's room was at the end, Avril's in the middle, so they stopped by a long window from where a rolling vista of cane-fields could be seen, part of Wayne's plantation.

"I never said he was in love with her."

Kerry felt at a loss. She could not discuss Wayne with her sister just now and she changed the subject, making casual conversation before bidding Avril good night and going along to her room.

All too soon it was Sunday. Instantly on waking Kerry's mind registered the fact that this was her last day. Tomorrow morning early she would be driven back to the hotel to begin work again. But the fleeting moment of blues was quickly replaced by a feeling of utter happiness as Kerry lay dwelling on Wayne's changed attitude towards her. Was he in love with her? Kerry felt sure he was, still considering his exclamation on the beach as a declaration of love. Why hadn't he told her categorically, though? Perhaps he had been going to do so yesterday, she thought, recalling that delicious moment when, finding himself alone with her for a few moments, Wayne had swept her into his arms and kissed her with an ardour that was both tempting and frightening.

"My delectable child! I want you!" She must resist him, was the desperate thought running through Kerry's mind as she gave ardent kiss for ardent kiss. Nothing must occur which could mar their future . . . or their wedding night. "Darling, will you –?" And, to Kerry's indescribable disappointment, her sister had entered the room. Never would Kerry have believed there would be an occasion when she would resent Avril's presence.

Just in time they had drawn apart; Kerry was fingering a magnificent Sung bowl when Avril entered, while Wayne was standing by the fireplace, one hand resting negligently on the mantelpiece. Had Wayne been going to propose? Kerry wondered again as she lay there, enjoying the luxury of her big bed, and the tropical sunshine pouring through the window. But of course he had! What else could he have been going to say in that moment of ecstatic intimacy? There was nothing.

Presently she rose and slid from the bed, slender and lovely, her hair tousled, her eyes dreamy – but not from sleep.

Breakfast was taken on the shady verandah, then she and Wayne and Avril went on to the beach, being joined a short while later by Rowena, sleek and lovely in her bikini, her hair loose on her shoulders, but she wasn't intending to get it wet, for in addition to the towel swinging from her hand she carried a bathing cap.

"Have you been in?" Rowena stood smiling down at Wayne. The two girls might not have been there for all the notice he took of them.

Wayne nodded absently, without even lifting his eyes.

"Can't she see we have?" scoffed Avril, flicking a spot

of water from one brown leg. Romena was walking towards the sea and after a while Wayne went in for another dip, leaving Kerry alone with her sister.

"I've been thinking," said Avril, her frowning gaze on the two who were now wading out into deeper water, "if Uncle Wayne marries that one I shall insist on returning to my own house. You could then come to live with me," she added, "and then I shouldn't miss Uncle Wayne so much." Avril's voice was a little flat, her eyes brooding as she scooped up a handful of silver sand and allowed it to trickle slowly through her fingers.

"I shouldn't meet trouble half way," was all Kerry could think of saying.

"What does he see in her?"

"She's very beautiful," was Kerry's automatic reply.

"But hard, as I said. No, he won't marry her," added Avril firmly, shaking her head to emphasize her words. "As I said before, I can only imagine Uncle Wayne with someone soft and pliable, and who loves him to distraction."

A rueful smile touched Kerry's lips. To think when last Avril had uttered similar words to these that she, Kerry, had actually felt sorry for any woman who loved Wayne to distraction!

"They're coming out. Now just you watch the way she looks at him – it's disgusting!"

"Disgusting?" A puzzled frown creased Kerry's brow, but a few moments later she knew exactly what her sister meant.

Wayne was dabbing himself with a towel and Rowena couldn't take her eyes off him; they moved in a prurient sort of way over his whole body – from his sinewed brown legs to his thighs and then to his chest, buried in thick brown hair. Strangely, they never settled on his

156

face, but Kerry's did, just to note his reaction. Either he was unaware of being the object of Rowena's attention, or he was determined to ignore it. Whatever he felt for Rowena, it certainly was not love. Kerry smiled at this deduction. How could he love Rowena when she herself had his love? Catching Kerry's eye, he smiled, in a tender way, and she heard a slight involuntary gasp at her side. What was Avril thinking? Kerry wondered, quite unable to turn and meet her sister's gaze.

Lunch time came and they all left the beach, strolling through the flower-filled garden to the house.

"Did you notice the way Uncle Wayne looked at you?" The words tumbled from Avril's lips the moment they were alone, outside her bedroom door. "Did you, Kerry?"

How she managed to produce an expression of mild surprise Kerry would never know.

"What do you mean, Avril?"

Bewilderedly Avril shook her head.

"He's never been interested in anyone except Rowena," she murmured just as if Kerry had not spoken. "He looked – he looked. . . ." Avril's lovely eyes were wide and still disbelieving. "Kerry, has it ever occurred to you that Uncle Wayne might be falling in love with you?"

Feigning mild surprise was one thing; to feign astonishment was by no means so simple. All the same, Kerry contrived to attain some semblance of it – although it did strike her that, very soon, Avril was going to accuse her of hypocrisy. Still, in the circumstances, Kerry could hardly be expected to confide her hopes – not until Wayne had spoken the words she longed to hear.

"Your uncle – love me?"

Avril was scanning Kerry's face as if seeing it for the first time, her eyes filled with admiration.

"He could, you know – oh, yes, indeed he could!"

"I seem to remember your emphatically declaring

you'd dislike anyone whom your uncle married," Kerry reminded Avril, more to hide her confusion than anything else.

"That –" Avril shrugged. "I never thought of you then."

To Kerry's relief the bell sounded for lunch and no more was said, both girls having to hurry to their respective rooms and change.

After lunch Avril and Rowena took their customary siesta while Kerry and Wayne relaxed on the lawn. The sun, almost directly overhead, shone from a sky flecked with sailing clouds, ferried by the trade wind. The air was laden with perfume, the immediate scene one of riotous colour as exotic blooms vied with each other in their flamboyant brilliance. One side of the lawn was banded with poinsettias, while the border was an interfusion of flaring tropical blooms backclothed by jacaranda and hibiscus. Further charm was added by glimpses of indigo sea, fringed with swaying coconut palms.

Presently Wayne spoke, saying he'd take Kerry out to dinner the following Wednesday. But as it transpired Wayne had a change of plan about the dinner; he told her only when they were in the car, driving away from the Beach Manor Hotel.

"We're dining at home. Avril has gone to visit friends and she'll be staying with them for a few days. As Miss Blakely is going out this evening we shall be on our own."

A tremor of excitement passed through Kerry, but she made no comment and they drove in silence for the rest of the way.

They ate at a table illuminated by candles, being served with delicious West Indian food and wine by a silent manservant, and afterwards Wayne surprised Kerry by suggesting that they retire to the drawing-room rather than the verandah, which was customary.

Shy, faintly uneasy, Kerry moved over to the lovely Sung bowl and stood looking down at it. Wayne watched her inscrutably for a long moment and then, moving over to her, he took her in his arms. But he neither spoke nor attempted to kiss her, and during those silent moments Kerry became aware of a sudden deflation of spirit, the cause of which was the intrusion into her memory of Charles's declaration that Wayne could never be true to one woman. Fear and entreaty dominated her expression as she lifted her eyes to meet his gaze. He was too handsome, too attractive in every way. What chance did she have?

"Darling! What on earth are you thinking to make you look like that?" His embrace was strong and reassuring and Kerry managed a shaky little laugh before she answered,

"It was nothing, Wayne – nothing important, that is."

"Your mind's not occupied with mundane things like money, I hope."

"Of course not. Why should it be?"

"I wondered if perhaps you were worrying about your financial problems."

A sudden quietude fell . . . over everything. Everything except Kerry's heart. It had a sledge-hammer impact on her ribs. For the question was wholly unnecessary – or should be.

"I'm not worrying about my financial problems," she trembled at last, through whitened lips.

Wayne frowned, and said,

"You mustn't, because from now on you won't have any."

"Not – not –" Kerry sagged. How silly she was! – which only went to prove that she had not been sure of Wayne, after all.

Drawing her to him, Wayne kissed away the last of her fears.

"We must see about that money you need for Michelle."

"Michelle!" Her eyes shone with gratitude. "Wayne, are you really concerned with Michelle?"

"Anything which concerns you concerns me from now on. Yes, you shall have the three thousand – quite soon."

"Soon...." With a deep sigh of thankfulness Kerry rested her head against his breast. "You haven't said anything to Avril yet," she murmured between his kisses, "because she hasn't mentioned anything about it to me."

"I intend giving it to you myself."

"You –?" Kerry struggled to put some small space between them, so that she could look up at Wayne. Love and deep gratitude shone in her eyes. "You're kind ... just as Avril said you were."

His glance was quizzical.

"It required Avril to tell you, naturally," he said with a laugh, and because she was so sure of him Kerry produced a little pout and looked injured and indignant.

"You hurt me," she complained.

"Much?"

"I expect it was my pride – mostly."

"I'm sorry, my darling. How could I have done that to you?"

Kerry did not want to talk about it and she snuggled close again, and after long moments of tender murmurings Wayne's voice suddenly became hoarse, his kisses more passionate and demanding. Dominated by his power, and the urgency of her own desire, Kerry fought against the helplessness assailing her. How did the Eve myth originate? she wondered, for it was the male – always it was the male who tempted, for the simple, primeval reason that his emotions were unhampered by fear.

"Wayne, let me go!" They were close to the couch.

Was it by some manoeuvre of his? Kerry began to struggle in earnest. "Darling, please!" she cried shakily. "Not until we're married. It would spoil everything –"

"Married!" Wayne's arms fell away from her, dropping to his sides. "Married?" he repeated, staring in disbelief. "Who said anything about marriage?"

Stunned, Kerry stared at him, like a disillusioned child, one tight little fist pressed to her mouth in an endeavour to stop its trembling.

"It – it w-wasn't m-marriage you – you ...?" Stupid words, but Kerry was trying, with a sort of frantic tenacity, to cling to her conviction that Wayne loved her, trying to reject the evidence of her ears. But memory brought back all her previous misgivings; they were fully explained now. Yet memory also brought a vision of that scene on the beach, when Wayne had treated her so tenderly, when she could have sworn the light in his eyes was kindled by love. He was standing close still and although her legs felt weak she managed to move away. Silence hung on the room, intense, like some all-pervading evil.

"If – if I can have my coat ...?" The humiliation was too much; Kerry turned from him, stumbling towards the door.

"Come back, Kerry." Wayne had hold of her again, but this time she disengaged herself with a savage twist of her body.

"Don't you dare touch me again!" Humility gave way to anger, which grew to a white-hot fury as she saw the mocking amusement appear in his eyes. "I now realize I'm just another woman to you – but to me you're – you're the dregs! Where's my coat!"

His expression changed; his dark eyes glinted dangerously.

"Why the act all at once? I've offered to be generous.

You shall have the three thousand –"

"Three thousand! Mr. Harvey, I'm not to be bought – like all your other women!" Her tear-filled eyes raked him with a contempt far in excess of his own. "Three thousand! Why pay so much? You could have a harem for that!" She spoke wildly, forgetting all about Avril, and that after this scene she would never be allowed to see her again. In any case, Kerry was making a mental vow that she would leave the island by the very next plane. "I asked for my coat!"

"A harem, eh?" he began, ignoring her request. "A harem – well, well."

Kerry made no response and for a long moment he stood there, regarding her silently, and with a most curious expression on his face. He seemed to be noting every single thing about her – the pallid cheeks and trembling lips, the heavily-misted eyes. Wordlessly she looked at him, her eyes moving from the frown lines on his brow to the unfamiliar greyness at the corners of his mouth, and then to the pulsating nerve in his throat.

"What gave you the idea I had marriage in mind?" he enquired softly, his eyes never leaving her face.

"I really wouldn't know," she flashed at him, "seeing that your disgusting reputation is known all over the island!"

"My –?" His eyes glinted dangerously. "You'll explain those words, if you please!"

This was not possible because, in her desire to hit back, she had exaggerated, lied even. A retraction she would never offer and with a swift escapist movement unanticipated by Wayne she tugged at the bell-rope.

"If you won't fetch my coat then someone else will." Her voice was quieter now, but her inner tumult still had a suffocating effect on her and she felt almost physically ill.

"Can you honestly deny you led me to believe –?"

"Led –?" Kerry stared, forgetful that her reciprocation on more than one occasion might have encouraged Wayne to assume she was "easy". "Oh, you shall not accuse me of that!" Wildly she looked round. Her rage having broken all bounds, she was deaf to Wayne's gasp as she made a grab at the Sung bowl. "You said my reactions disappointed you – well, I hope you're not disappointed this time!"

"Kerry, put that down! Put it *down*! You don't know its value –"

His hand shot out as the bowl which had survived for a thousand years went hurtling across the room. It hit the cut-glass shade of the standard lamp; a shattering ring filled the room before the fragments dropped soundlessly on to the carpet.

In the awful silence that ensued all that really struck Kerry was the blood spurting from Wayne's wrist and the appearance of a dusky figure in the doorway.

Entering the room, Cecilia stood there, gaping.

"Massa Harvey, you're hurt – but da bowl! Da beautiful bowl dat you only just bought last month! – and dat you say only Cecilia must dust. . . ." Crossing the room, she knelt down and picked up several pieces of the broken pottery, the relatively unimportant matter of Wayne's injury forgotten. "Da bowl dat Missy Avril say cost you nearly two thousand pounds –"

"Two th-thousand p-pounds?" A trembling hand stole to Kerry's cheek.

"What happened, Massa Harvey? Dat you was careless is for sure!"

Kerry's frightened eyes moved to Wayne. Having taken a handkerchief from his pocket he was binding up his wound, his unmoving gaze fixed on Kerry's face. He appeared so cool and unaffected by the breakage that

Kerry began to wonder if Cecilia had made a mistake over the price paid for the bowl. Her glance shifted to Cecilia; she asked the girl to fetch her coat. At the quietly-spoken request Cecilia straightened up, looking first at Kerry, then at Wayne, and lastly at the broken blue pottery scattered about the carpet. And then her eyes became enormous as the truth hit her.

"Missy," she murmured in an awed voice. "Missy go and chuck da bowl at da massa!"

Wayne was looking over Cecilia's head and Kerry turned, the colour rushing back into her cheeks as she saw Rowena standing in the doorway, and realized that she had overheard what Cecilia had just said.

"Wayne! What on earth's happened? The Sung – and you having it only a month, and wanting it long? What happened?" she said again, her glance taking in Kerry's hot face and the improvised bandage on Wayne's wrist.

Kerry's mouth tightened. The girl was thoroughly enjoying the situation!

"Why the question, Miss Blakely? You heard what Cecilia said." Cecilia, Kerry noticed, had left the room; she came back directly with Kerry's coat. "Thank you, Cecilia." Taking it from her, Kerry left the room. Seconds later the front door closed quietly behind her.

CHAPTER X

IMMEDIATELY after breakfast the following morning Kerry cabled her father. He should be back in England now and Kerry was sure he would loan her the money for her fare home. With any luck she would be off the island within a few days. Although unhappy at the idea of leav-

164

ing without saying goodbye to Avril, Kerry hoped she
would be away before her sister's return to the Trade
Winds Estate. It would then be Wayne's task to explain
Kerry's sudden departure. How he would contrive to do
this without revealing his own dastardly behaviour Kerry
neither knew nor cared, but that he would invent some
excuse for the disappearance of the Sung bowl she did
not doubt; she was also convinced that he would forbid
either Rowena or Cecilia to mention the "row" which
had taken place between Kerry and himself.

This supposition was proved to be correct later when
Kerry received a telephone call from Wayne, at the sound
of whose voice Kerry had the suffocating sensation of her
heart beating right up in her throat as for one wild moment she deceived herself into believing he had rung to
express remorse, and to arrange a meeting between them.

"Miss Fairclough speaking . . . Kerry. . . ."

"It's about Avril; it is not my wish that she should learn
of our – disagreement." Curt accents, unfriendly and cold.
Kerry sagged with sheer desolation; tears stung her eyes.

"The task of explaining will be yours, Mr. Harvey.
I'm expecting to leave Barbados before Avril returns to
your house."

"Leave?" sharply. "You're leaving the island?"

"That's my intention."

"Avril –" He seemed perturbed now and his voice had
lost its hostile edge. "She'll be upset if you leave."

"I shall write to her when I get home."

A long silence and then,

"What excuse will you offer for your hasty departure?"
At this question Kerry's blood boiled; she was seized with
an overwhelming desire to leave him in suspense.

"I shall probably tell her the truth! It seems to me that
it's high time Avril learned what you really are! Yes, I
think I shall write her a long letter revealing what an

unutterable cad you are!" And, without giving him an opportunity to speak Kerry said she was busy and rang off. Would he ring again? she wondered. But as the afternoon progressed she realized he had not taken her threat seriously. She and he had one thing in common: neither would deliberately hurt Avril, and Wayne knew that Kerry would think up some other excuse for her departure from the island. This problem occupied Kerry's mind for the next couple of days, but was to be solved in a way that only added to Kerry's troubles, yet made her forget her own deep hurt in her anxiety for Michelle.

The party including Irene and Stan arrived during the late afternoon, crowding into the hotel, so that Kerry was too busy to talk to Irene and there was time only for snatched greetings between the two girls before, having arranged to meet Kerry in the lounge after dinner, Irene and Stan were whisked away to their room by the waiting porter.

Scarcely able to contain her impatience now that Irene was here, Kerry found the time dragging until at last she was crossing the lounge to the table by the window at which Irene and Stan were seated. Rising as she approached, Stan asked what she was drinking, and even as he was ordering, Kerry, struck at once by the gravity of her friend's expression, asked in a breathless tone,

"Michelle ... you have something important to tell me?"

"It isn't Michelle, but her father," Irene replied at once. "I expect she told you he was in hospital –?"

"In hospital?" Kerry shook her head, thinking back to Michelle's last letter and the omission of her customary detailed account of how she had spent the money Kerry had sent to her. Kerry now saw that it had gone on such things as flowers and fruit to take to the hospital. "No, she never mentioned it."

Irene's face creased in a frown, then cleared.

"I expect she didn't want to cause you anxiety."

"Is it serious?"

Irene and Stan exchanged glances.

"As serious as it can be." A grave pause while the waiter placed their drinks on the table. "There's no hope at all for him."

Kerry stared, her heart missing a beat.

"He's dying?"

"Three weeks ago he was given a month to live – a month at the most." This significant statement was followed by a moment's silence as Kerry tried to take it in.

"But ... how awful!" Her face was white; leaning across his wife, Stan picked up Kerry's glass and held it out to her.

"Have a drink, Kerry. You look as if you need one."

"Thank you." Accepting the glass from Stan, Kerry held it to her lips. "It's very strange that Michelle could write like that – I mean, I sensed something – but there was no underlying hint of tragedy in her letter."

"Neither Michelle nor her mother knew the seriousness of the situation at that time – and perhaps Michelle doesn't know even now." Irene went on to explain how the knowledge had come to her. She had met a friend, Rosemary Hall, on the bus. Having recently finished her training Rosemary was now a nurse at the Baronsfield Hospital. Being new to the job she had been full of it, describing the various cases, and emphasizing the plight of one poor woman with six children whose widowhood was imminent, her husband being in hospital with a heart complaint. "I wasn't really taking much notice," Irene admitted, giving her approaching wedding as an excuse. "However, when she let fall the name of the man – Mr. Johnson, I did sit up and take notice, as you can well imagine, and after putting a few questions to Rosemary

I soon had enough information to realize that this Mr. Johnson was Michelle's father. I asked if the mother knew of the danger and Rosemary said she hadn't yet been told because up till the previous day the doctors had held out some hope of prolonging Mr. Johnson's life." Irene paused to take a drink and Kerry's eyes moved abstractedly to Stan. He was being left out of the conversation and it struck Kerry that on this the first evening of his marriage, he must be wishing her miles away. "I didn't tell you anything in my letter," Irene was saying, "because somehow I felt it would be less of a blow if you actually heard it."

"I'm glad you did leave it," murmured Kerry, and, after a pensive silence, "I wonder what poor Mrs. Johnson will do now?"

"At least she won't be having more babies," intervened Stan in a dry and faintly amused tone.

"The financial aspect," Kerry pointed out, troubled. "Mrs. Johnson's relief will be cut. They'll be poorer than ever." Kerry's hand went to her stomach; it was an involuntary gesture, for she felt empty inside – almost physically sick, in fact. She could see no future at all for Michelle. The child would never contemplate leaving Mrs. Johnson now; Kerry accepted this fact. Michelle would consider it her duty to help her mother in this time of struggle and stress.

"Tell me about Avril," Irene invited, with the obvious intention of steering on to a happier trend of conversation.

But to her amazement Kerry's eyes filled up.

"That isn't right, either." Instantly the admission was out Kerry regretted it. She should not be sharing her troubles with Irene on this her wedding night. But it was too late; Irene's interest and curiosity were fully awakened and even a small sigh from her husband did not deter her from saying,

"What do you mean? From your last letter I gathered everything was just fine."

Kerry shook her head; it was a despairing gesture, a gesture of abandoned hope which seemed to shock Irene.

"Kerry, what is it?"

"I c-can't tell you, Irene. It's your wedding day. Oh, I'm selfish!" She made to rise, but Irene laid a restraining hand on her arm.

"I'm your friend, Kerry. It might be my wedding day, but I fail to see what difference that makes. If you feel like talking, then I'm ready to listen."

"Stan –" she murmured, but he interrupted her, saying gently,

"Don't worry about me, Kerry. Unburden yourself; you'll feel much better for it." He smiled at his wife. "I'll take a stroll in the grounds, if you don't mind?"

"Thanks, darling. Just leave us for about ten minutes or so."

Kerry watched him go, trying not to envy her friend, and yet thinking of Wayne . . . and what might have been. Might . . .? Why speculate on the impossible? Wayne Harvey was a confirmed bachelor – but even if he were not he would never choose a girl like Kerry for a wife. He would look for sophistication and poise, choose a woman with a personality matching his own – no matter what Avril had said about "someone soft and pliable . . . who would love him to distraction".

"Spill it, Kerry," encouraged Irene, and after the merest hesitation Kerry related all that had happened. After undergoing several changes as Kerry's story progressed, Irene's expression became set in lines of angry indignation. "He's really led you to believe he meant marriage?"

"I don't know – not now. He said once – to the proprietor here, who's a friend of his – that he'd a built-in protection against marriage. I didn't take that seriously enough."

"Built-in protection?" Irene's brows were raised. "Sounds a pompous ass to me. If he ever does marry I hope he gets a bitch who'll lead him the dance he deserves! He sounds absolutely abominable! – and frankly, I don't know how you could have fallen for him in the first place."

Despite her misery Kerry had to smile at that.

"You haven't seen him, Irene," was her brief reply.

"Nor do I want to – no, on second thoughts I'd love to see him – just to give the bounder a piece of my mind!"

After a long while Kerry said,

"You won't mention this to Stan? I don't want anyone else to know how stupid I am."

"I won't say a word." Irene paused, anxiously scanning her friend's face. "What are your plans?"

"I've cabled to Father asking him for the money for my fare home."

Irene frowned.

"Where will you live?" Angrily she shook her head. "If only I hadn't given up the flat. Will you be able to live with one of your parents?"

"I might be able to stay with Father for a week, just while I find a room –"

"A room! One room? It won't come to that?"

"I'm determined to give Mrs. Johnson all I can."

"Her problems aren't yours, Kerry," said Irene gently, but Kerry was shaking her head.

"It's for Michelle, obviously. I must try to make things easier for her."

Irene drew an angry breath.

"I wish with all my heart you'd never seen that damned money! It's ruined your whole life!"

"Hardly my whole life," Kerry returned, though in a flat and hopeless tone. "I'll get over Wayne, and the rest will also sort itself out with time."

"A long time! And if you don't mind my blunt speaking, I'm not at all enamoured with Avril. If she really wanted to she could insist on helping Michelle. She could, even at this stage, cough up that three thousand to buy that business –"

"What good would that be now?"

"Mrs. Johnson could manage it – with paid help."

"Yes, of course. I never thought of that." Kerry spoke automatically, then realized the words were wasted. The three thousand would never now be forthcoming, she thought, a flush rising as she remembered Wayne's offer . . . and what he expected in return for his money.

"If you ask me," Irene was continuing, just as if Kerry had never spoken, "Avril's utterly selfish –"

"No, Irene, she isn't. But Wayne has full control of her money. She was only biding her time before asking for the air fare to bring Michelle out for a holiday. You see, she had no idea of what was developing between Wayne and me."

"The air fare?" repeated Irene. "Is that all? Why not the three thousand?"

"Avril didn't know about it. I told Wayne, but not Avril." Kerry frowned at Irene's expression. "You're wrong about Avril. She's sweet – truly."

Irene ignored that.

"Does she know you're leaving the island?"

"Not yet." Kerry explained about Avril's being away for a few days. "I was wondering what excuse to give her for my hasty decision, but now I can write from England and say it's because of Michelle's father."

"She'll expect you to come back, though."

"Yes. But that won't matter. I'll just keep putting it off."

"In other words, you don't care if you eventually lose touch with Avril?"

Kerry sighed.

"I don't want to lose touch, Irene – but yes, I think that eventually I'll stop writing. It's for the best. You see, Avril loves Wayne dearly; she's known him all her life. Me –" Kerry shrugged. "She's not known me long enough to become really close –"

"You wrote as though you were really close," Irene cut in to remind Kerry.

"It seemed as if we were, but now – Oh, I don't know," cried Kerry in despair. "I don't know how the whole thing's going to end!"

"That legacy!" exclaimed Irene in disgust.

"It brought me Michelle."

"Michelle," Irene repeated impatiently. "It looks as if she's going to be a burden to you for some considerable time. Oh, I'd say nothing if you'd been brought up with her – but to think only a few months ago you didn't even know her. And now you're facing a spate of trouble and anxiety that ought not to be yours at all."

"Michelle's very sweet, Irene."

"Like Avril," with heavy sarcasm, and Kerry frowned. "You could have done very well without either of them!"

Stan returned and Kerry rose instantly.

"Good night," she smiled, and had moved away even before they answered her.

On her way upstairs she met Charles. She had told him she would be leaving, and although he was far from pleased, mainly because she was not giving him reasonable notice, he had now reverted to his former attitude of cordiality.

"Going to bed?" he queried in surprise. "At this time?"

172

She nodded.

"I'm tired."

"You've been talking to your friends, I noticed."

"Just for a few minutes," she replied, and Charles grinned.

"We have two honeymoon couples in, so we must think of something."

"Think of something?"

"Push a subtle hint into the cabaret one night."

"I don't think my friends will be pleased if everyone gets to know they're on their honeymoon."

"Everyone won't get to know. They'll hear just enough to arouse their curiosity – set them guessing, as it were." Charles stayed chatting for a few minutes and then, after Kerry had refused to accompany him to the bar for a drink, he said good night and let her go.

Three days later Kerry was on the plane, misery clawing at her heart. Somehow, despite the fact that she repeatedly told herself Wayne was a cad and a profligate, and that she was far better off without him, an insistent ember of expectancy had been kept burning right up to the moment when, after saying goodbye to Charles, Kerry had got into the car which her friends had hired, and been driven by Stan away from the Beach Manor Hotel.

Only then had hope flickered out. Irene had chatted all the way to the airport, trying to cheer Kerry up, undoubtedly, but without much success. However, Kerry did manage a smile at the moment of parting and the last thing Irene and Stan did was to tell her that they would be in touch immediately they arrived home, and she must come and visit them the following week-end.

The plane was airborne and Kerry glanced down; but cloud hung low and soon they had glided right into it. As the island became lost to view Kerry thought of that other flight, and her arrival at Barbados. So optimistic she had been, looking excitedly towards the future when Michelle would be released through the kindness and generosity of Avril, and all three would meet in one wonderful never-to-be-forgotten reunion. Little did she know then how soon her happiness and optimism were to be shattered, or of the trouble she was to encounter almost immediately on landing on the island.

Kerry's father met her at the airport, and seeing him looking well and fit lent a ray of lightness to her heart. He was glad to see her and when she asked if she could stay with him and his wife until she found suitable accommodation he readily agreed.

As he had been out of England for practically the whole of Kerry's stay on Barbados, he hadn't received any news from Kerry, and so he wanted to know all about Avril and her guardian.

Kerry obliged, watching his eyes open wide as she described both Avril's plantation house and Wayne's.

"Real wealth, by the sound of it. Lucky girl!"

"Yes, far luckier than Michelle. I told you a little about Michelle before I went away – about the poverty in which she lived." Kerry now went on to tell him about Mr. Johnson; he gave a few "tut tuts" in between concentrating on his driving and, seeing that he was not in the least interested, Kerry ceased going into details and ended by saying, "I wrote to Michelle telling her I'd be back in England today, and that I'd go and see her tomorrow afternoon."

Michelle opened the door to Kerry, and flung herself into her arms.

"Oh, I'm so glad you're back! I was beginning to think I'd never see you again and then, yesterday morning, I received your letter. I just couldn't believe it, because even though you said you'd come for a holiday next year I thought you'd love that beautiful island so much that you'd decide to stay there for ever! Why did you decide to come back? Were you homesick?" Kerry just nodded; that was as good an excuse as any.

"Come on in," Michelle continued, flushed with excitement. "What am I doing, keeping you in the lobby!" She was laughing and crying at the same time and Kerry herself felt a prick of tears behind her eyes as she followed Michelle into the sitting-room. It was good to be back with Michelle. Much as she loved Avril, Kerry was beginning to wonder if she had her values right. Irene had suggested that Avril could have done something for Michelle, and Kerry was now finding herself in agreement with Irene, for Avril did have a way with her uncle and Kerry felt sure that, had she pressed him, she would quite soon have managed to get her own way. Well, that was all in the past. It was most unlikely that Avril would bother her head about Michelle now that Kerry was no longer there to remind Avril of her young sister's plight. The practical thing to do was for Kerry to get work at once so that she could continue to assist Michelle and her mother.

"Where is everybody?" Kerry spoke guardedly, remembering she was not supposed to know that Mr. Johnson was in hospital. "The little ones . . .?"

"Janice from next door came and took them to the park – because I said you were coming and her mother said she was sure we'd like an hour on our own. Wasn't that nice of her? The neighbours have been wonderful during – during. . . ." Michelle trailed off, flushing hotly. "Kerry, I – I didn't tell you in my letter because I didn't want to upset you – but Father's in hospital." Pausing, she glanced anxiously at Kerry, who instantly smiled, and Michelle's face cleared. "Mother's at the hospital. She always

goes on Saturday and Sunday afternoons – and Wednesdays. But on Wednesdays she only has half an hour with
Father because if she took the whole afternoon off work
she wouldn't get paid. If she takes only an hour off her
boss doesn't stop any money. The hospital's not far from
her work, so she can get there in a quarter of an hour."
Michelle was excited, and not unduly anxious about her
father. It was obvious that she had not yet been enlight-
ened as to the seriousness of his condition. "Sit down,
Kerry, and I'll make some tea and while we're drinking
it you can tell me all about Avril. Oh, I know you told
me lots in your letters, but I want to know everything –
every single detail about her. I lie in bed and think about
her and imagine I'm going on a visit to her. Do you think
I ever will?"

Kerry swallowed hard, hating Wayne Harvey and his
meanness and over-protective attitude regarding Avril's
money.

"Of course you will, Michelle dear."

"We'll go together for a holiday – you and I?" the
small piquant face was aglow with anticipation. Kerry's
heart was like lead as she pictured Michelle's future. But
she said, in soft and gentle tones,

"Yes, Michelle, we'll go together some time." She sat
down and Michelle disappeared into the kitchen. "Can
I do anything?" Kerry inquired after a few minutes.

"Nothing. I've had the kettle on and off the boil for
ages – it's boiling again now. Biscuits or cake?"

About to refuse anything to eat, Kerry asked for a bis-
cuit, it suddenly occurring to her that these luxuries had
been bought especially for her. "You still have the lady
to come in and clean?" she asked, looking around.

"She comes only twice a week now." Michelle stood
with the tray in her hand, looking faintly apologetic.
"You see, we had to spend some of the money on things

for Father. There are the bus fares to the hospital, for one thing. It's awfully expensive when we go from here – because it's a long way. And sometimes the children go – not all of them, of course. Only the two eldest. Mother didn't like to spend your money in this way, but I told her you wouldn't mind in the least." Kerry said nothing; she had sent the money for a daily help simply to save Michelle from slaving away at the housework. Still, under the present circumstances she could hardly begin complaining that the money wasn't being spent as she intended. "It'll be all right again when Father comes out of hospital. Mrs. Furness is quite willing to come in more often just as soon as we can afford it."

So Michelle believed her father would soon be out of hospital!

Sighing, Kerry asked who was now minding the children during the day.

"I've had to stay off school."

Kerry frowned. What was to happen when Mr. Johnson died? His widow would have to stay at home. But somehow Kerry was convinced that she would continue working if she possibly could – and not only because of the money. She had once told Kerry that going out to work was far more enjoyable than minding the babies.

Michelle had gone into the kitchen to make a pot of tea and Kerry moved over to the window. The back "garden" was a mere patch of earth compressed to the hardness of concrete by the human traffic continually passing over it. A dusty sparse hedge of privet divided it from a similar patch of ground next door. In one corner stood two plastic dustbins minus their lids and in another an empty dog kennel with rotting sides and a rusty chain lying along the ground beside it.

"Tea's ready." Michelle was still bright and her eager pleasure at seeing Kerry again was like balm to a wound.

Someone cared. . . . With firm resolve Kerry determined to put the whole of Barbados behind her and devote herself to Michelle and her mother. Here she could do some good, and perhaps in this way her own heartache would gradually fade. Avril would forget her quite soon, for her life was full and satisfying – with her friends and her wealth and the uncle who loved her. Yes, however shallow his way with other women, Wayne Harvey did care for his niece.

"Shall I pour the tea?" Kerry asked as Michelle placed the tray on the table and sat down.

"Yes, please. And tell me all about Avril!" Michelle urged, her eyes shining and expectant. "I kept wondering if she would write to me, but she didn't. Perhaps she's very busy, though."

Sudden bitterness flooded over Kerry. She and Avril had discussed the possibility of Avril starting a correspondence with Michelle, but Avril had been reluctant to do so, saying the time wasn't right yet, because of course Wayne hadn't been "softened up" – as Avril termed it – until the day of Kerry's visit. It wasn't as if she could keep the correspondence a secret, Avril had said, which was quite true because, as Wayne had previously told Kerry, all the mail came either to him or Rowena. Kerry was just becoming worried about an explanation as to why Avril had not written when Michelle's voice broke into her thoughts, again pressing for information about her sister.

"Tell me what she's like! I know she's beautiful, because of the snapshots you sent me. But you never sent me any of her house. Have you got some of that?"

"Yes, Michelle, I have." No use trying to fob the child off; she was highly intelligent and would know very well that Kerry must have taken photographs of her sister's house.

"It's – it's a mansion!" exclaimed Michelle in an awed voice. She could not take her eyes off the picture Kerry had handed to her. "Is this her very own house?"

"Her very own, Michelle. Her parents were exceedingly rich."

At last Michelle placed the snapshot on the table.

"I'd love to go and see it for myself." Her eyes were dreamy; there was no trace of envy in her voice, just a faint sadness and longing. "It will be years and years before I can go to Barbados, won't it, Kerry?"

"Perhaps it will be a long while," Kerry reluctantly agreed, but added, "We'll go, though; haven't we said we'll have a holiday together on Barbados some day?"

Michelle brightened; her lovely eyes regained the sparkle Kerry had seen on first entering the house.

"Of course – and it's something to look forward to." Michelle glanced at the clock; it was about the third or fourth time she had done so and this time she made some small remark about her mother being late, adding that she must have decided to do some shopping on the way home. "What's Avril's house like inside?" Questions and more questions, which Kerry answered, knowing the child would not envy her sister. Nevertheless, Kerry was careful not to lay undue stress on the wealth and luxury that surrounded her. As she listened Michelle's glance strayed to the clock again, an action that set Kerry's nerves on edge. Michelle's next words, as she changed the subject, did not help. "Where on earth can Mother be?"

"What time does she usually get back?"

"About four. Visiting time on Saturday is from two till three. It's now a quarter to five."

"You said she might have decided to do some shopping," Kerry reminded her.

"It wouldn't take all this time. Besides –" Michelle shook her head – "there's very little she can do; we got all the weekend groceries in this morning and we haven't much money left."

"Well, don't worry, Michelle. I expect there's some explanation for her lateness." But Kerry's nerves were fluttering and she wondered if it would be kinder to give Michelle some hint of the true position regarding her father. However, Michelle began to question Kerry again, this time about the hotel in which she had worked, and about the island itself. Then Kerry helped her with the washing up and by this time it was five-thirty and the children were just racing across the tiny back garden. A girl of about fourteen parked the pram, kicked at the brake, then came across to the window.

"Your sister came, then," she observed unnecessarily, staring at Kerry.

"Yes. Are you coming in to be introduced?"

"Do it through the window."

Michelle looked apologetically at her sister, but made the introduction all the same.

"Pleased to meet you," smiled Kerry. "It's good of you to have the children."

"They weren't much trouble today." Janice turned her attention to Michelle. "I'll have them for an hour to-morrow if you want to visit your dad."

"Thanks, Janice. Yes, I shall be going to see Father."

"How is he today? Mum'll be asking."

"I don't know how he is. Mother's not back yet."

"Not back? Thought she always caught the half-past three bus."

"She normally does; I can't think what's happened."

"I expect she got talking to some of the other visitors and missed the bus. 'Bye!"

"Goodbye – and thank you, Janice."

"You're welcome." The rusty iron gate clanged behind Janice; the four children came bounding in, ravenous.

"I'll have to get their tea." Another apologetic glance for Kerry. "Sit down – on the big chair; then I can feed them at the table."

"Let me help you. I'd much rather."

"Oh –" Michelle flushed at the idea of Kerry helping her. "No, I can manage."

"It will be done in half the time if I help." Kerry was already in the kitchen and she glanced round. "What are they having?"

"Toast and jam. Baby will have a bottle – he's had a bad tummy lately and brings everything up except milk."

"You see to his bottle, then, and while I make the toast –" Kerry broke off as she saw Mrs. Johnson coming through the gate through which Janice had passed a moment ago. "Your – your mother's back," she whispered. The woman walked unsteadily, a handkerchief to her eyes. . . .

"I've never felt so utterly helpless and frustrated," Kerry was saying to her father later that evening. "Mrs. Johnson insists on carrying on with her work – says she couldn't bear to stop at home. She intends using any money I can provide to pay some neighbour to have the children until four in the afternoons. Michelle will then pick them up on her way from school, give them their tea, clean the house, get the meal for her mother and herself – it's dreadful. I can't bear to think of it. Why can't Mrs. Johnson stop at home? They're her children, and she should look after them!"

"I understand your distress," her father returned mildly, glancing at his wife as she gave an impatient sigh. "But it's hardly your affair –"

"And it certainly isn't ours," his wife intervened with an indifferent glance in Kerry's direction. "You're not expecting your father to help, I hope."

Kerry sagged, and without another word, went up to the room she had been given. But she paced the floor, thinking of Avril, and how easily everything could be resolved if only Wayne would let her part with three thousand pounds. For Mrs. Johnson had mentioned the business – which was still for sale – saying that had Kerry been able to produce the money for it then she, Mrs. Johnson, would have been able to pay for all the help that was required, both in the house and the shop. And, Mrs. Johnson had added significantly, Michelle could have gone to live with Kerry.

Three thousand – and Avril probably worth a quarter of a million! Should she write to Avril? But Kerry dismissed the idea instantly, convinced that any letter she sent would never come into her sister's hands.

Kerry managed to get a job within a week and on the third morning she was seated at her desk when just before lunch a telephone call was put through for her.

It was Stephen Haslett, asking if she could be at his office at three o'clock that afternoon.

Kerry's heartbeats quickened.

"Is something wrong? What –?"

"I never go into details over the telephone, Miss Fairclough, as you know from experience. I'll expect you at three, then?" He had got her place of work from Michelle, he added.

"No – er – I've just started a new job," Kerry began, when he interrupted her.

"It's vitally important that you be in my office at three." Before Kerry could get in another word the line went dead.

"I can't ask for time off," she muttered to herself. "Not when I've only just started."

But of course she did, and as her new boss saw at once that the matter must be important he said she could leave the office at two-thirty.

At ten minutes to three Kerry arrived at the solicitor's office and was immediately shown into Stephen Haslett's private room.

"What is it?" she asked breathlessly, even before the door had closed behind the clerk.

"No need for anxiety, Miss Fairclough," replied Stephen Haslett. "Do sit down."

"But –"

"At three o'clock your visitor will be here; as we've a little time to spare I might as well do a spot of explaining." He stopped, indicating the chair again and Kerry sat down. Why doesn't he get on with it? she fumed, even more dazed by the mention of a visitor. "Over a week ago your sister's uncle, Wayne Harvey, having got my address from some friends of yours holidaying in Barbados, wrote informing me that he was coming to England and requested me to arrange a meeting between you and him. No, Miss Fairclough, please don't interrupt. As I happened to be away on holiday, and as my father was off work with a slight indisposition, the letter did not receive attention until this morning. You can imagine my surprise on reading it, because I'd been informed by Mick that you were intending remaining in Barbados for some time. I had only just put the letter down when Mr. Harvey and his niece called. We talked at some length –"

"Talked?" interrupted Kerry. "What about?"

A strange smile hovered on Stephen Haslett's lips for a space and then,

"We had a long talk, Miss Fairclough, let's leave it at that. To continue: I had already told Mr. Harvey that I didn't have your address in England but said I could get it from Mr. Johnson, Michelle's father, who would be sure to be at home. I believed he would have your address because, seeing that you were back here, you would be

183

visiting Michelle. Mr. Harvey then surprised me by saying he would come with me as he wanted to meet this Mr. Johnson, although he didn't go into details as to the reason – at least, not at that time, but he did later." Stephen moved over to a chair and sat down. The pause provided Kerry with the opportunity of saying something, but by now she was far too interested to interrupt Stephen's flow of information. "Well, we had hardly knocked on the Johnson door when a neighbour appeared with all the latest news. Mr. Johnson was dead, his wife had resumed her work, the children were being minded by another neighbour, and Michelle was at school. After she had given us the name of the school we went there and –" He stopped and looked kindly at Kerry. "The reunion took place in the headmistress's office – and tearful it was, too," he added with wry humour. "Even the dour headmistress was almost at breaking point, while the two strong men gulped and swallowed and sighed with relief when the headmistress suggested we take Michelle home, which we did."

"You took Mr. Harvey to that house?"

"Michelle made us some tea and we stayed a while, talking. Then Mr. Harvey and I came away."

"Where is Avril now?"

"Still there. Mr. Harvey said he'd pick her up later. He wants to see Michelle's mother."

Kerry was silent a long while, digesting all this. Was it Avril's doing – or Wayne's. If it were Wayne's – Kerry thrust away the idea that set her heart racing. Avril must have got round her uncle and persuaded him to help Michelle. . . . But for Wayne to come to England personally to conduct business that could have been done through a lawyer? It wasn't feasible. Of course! Kerry had it now. The sole reason they were here was because Avril wanted to meet Michelle; yes, that was it. Kerry frowned at the muddle of her thoughts. For she was now confronted with the fact that Wayne had expressly asked Stephen to arrange a meeting between himself and Kerry – here in Stephen Haslett's office. What did Wayne want with her? The heavy chimes of the wall clock actually making her jump, Kerry rose to her feet.

"Mr. Haslett, I don't want –" The phone rang; Stephen picked it up.

"Show him in," he said abruptly, and Kerry took a faltering step towards the door between Stephen's office and that of his father.

"I don't want to meet – to meet. . . ." Her voice trailed away into silence as Wayne entered. Tall and composed as ever, he stood a moment near the door. And now Kerry noticed the slight pallor under the tan of his cheeks, the uncontrollable movement of a nerve in his throat.

"I'll leave you," obliged Stephen in an expressionless voice. But at the door he turned. "I have another client in an hour," he said, and went out, closing the door softly behind him.

For what seemed an eternity Wayne and Kerry stood there, regarding one another. Kerry tried several times to speak – and in fact her lips did frame the words, "Why have you come?" but there was no sound and for the next few minutes emotion held her tongue-tied. Wayne too seemed unable to speak, and although by now Kerry's heart was telling her why he was here, her mind told her that if he had come because he loved her then he would have no difficulty in expressing that love. He said at last, making no move to approach her,

"Kerry. . . ." The clarity of his voice was lacking, the familiar hardness of his eyes was tempered by remorse. "Kerry, my dear, can you forgive me?"

"Forgive?" Even now the words she wanted to say eluded her. "You mean – you want us to be friends again

– for Avril's sake?" Avril had been fretting. The explanation intruded, cruel and remorseless, stealing away hope. He had come to ask for friendship, not love. "It is because of Avril, isn't it?" Like a bewildered child she looked at him, her eyes far too bright, her mouth quivering.

"Not because of Avril." He took a step towards her, then stopped. "I've been a fool, Kerry. And for a whole week after you'd left the island I fought and fought to hold on to my freedom. Marriage was not for me, I had decided long ago." He came to her at last, and took both her hands in his. She looked up at his chiselled features, trembling at his touch, and fired as before by his strength and magnetism and the power he had over her emotions. His eyes looked deeply into hers as he said, "I know now that the last thing I want is my freedom." Her hands were released as his arms slid about her. "Will you be my wife, Kerry?" His voice pleaded in a way that did not suit him at all. "You must, my darling, for I know I can't live without you!"

Words she had longed to hear, yet a chill swept through her and she shuddered against his body.

"It's because I wouldn't – wouldn't –" Kerry broke off, but despite her embarrassment she managed to look into his eyes. "It's only because you want me, isn't it?" Kerry thought he winced at her words, but could not be sure.

"You're trying to say that could I have had you without it I would never have offered marriage?"

"It's obvious," she answered, a little break in her voice.

Wayne's eyes never wavered from her face as he said,

"Kerry darling, that's not the reason I want to marry you. I admit I thought it would be enough, even though I knew I loved you –"

"Loved me?" She stared at him, bewildered. "But you didn't love me."

"I loved you, Kerry. I was also sure you loved me, and

186

knew in my heart that, if we did have an affair, it would be for all time; that was why I said you must never worry your head about money from now on. Yes, my darling, you were right when you assumed that I loved you. But like a damned fool I believed I could dispense with marriage. Well, I can't. I'm no superior being, after all." He held her from him and she thrilled to the tenderness she saw in his eyes. "Darling, you haven't said you forgive me."

A smile quivered; Kerry touched his lips with her fingers.

"It's all finished with," she murmured, but her hand was caught by Wayne's and held against his chest.

"I must hear it, sweetheart. Say you forgive me for hurting you so abominably."

"Must I?" She smiled lovingly at him. "All right, I forgive you."

"I swear I'll never hurt you again." His voice was low and ardently vibrating. "Never, my darling!"

"I know you won't – Oh, Wayne, you're hurting me already!" But her cry of protest went unheard as Wayne swept her into a crushing embrace, almost swinging her off her feet by his ardour and his strength. His mouth on hers was hard, possessive; Kerry gasped for breath when at last he released her.

"I'll get a special licence and we'll be married right away," he declared, in that proprietorial manner which had thrilled her once before. "Will that suit you?"

A smile curved Kerry's lips as for one humorous moment she wondered what would happen were she to say no, it didn't suit her. However, as she wholeheartedly agreed with the arrangement she merely replied,

"It will suit me very well."

His gaze became quizzical.

"Rather stiff, isn't it?"

She laughed then and found herself caught in his arms again. But a treacherous stab of memory brought back Charles's voice saying that Wayne could never be faithful to one woman, and in her near-panic Kerry said without thinking,

"Wayne, are you quite sure you want to marry me?"

"I thought we'd settled all that." It was plain that he had missed the tiny hint of fear in her voice. "Of course I want to marry you –" He looked down; she noticed the quirk of amusement at the corners of his mouth as he added, "I did have one or two qualms about acquiring a wife who threw Sung bowls at me. However, I decided I could just about afford it."

The colour rushed to Kerry's face.

"You'll never forgive me," she cried, and when no comment was forthcoming she added, "Was it really worth all that money?"

"Afraid so."

"Oh, dear," she said with contrition, but immediately added, "You shouldn't have provoked me."

"No, darling, I shouldn't," Wayne readily agreed. "And I do assure you I'll never provoke you again – at least," he amended, "not if there are any Sung bowls lying around."

"It isn't anything to laugh about. I'll never get it off my mind."

"I hope you will, my love. There are other things I'm expecting you to have on your mind!"

She laughed and heard him catch his breath before she said, becoming serious again,

"Can't the bowl be repaired?"

"I've sent it away to London. It will come back looking exactly as it was."

"It will?" Relief swept through her. "They can make it perfect again?"

Wayne shook his head.

"An expert would be able to spot the repair at once."

"So its value really has gone?"

"Most of it, yes – Don't look so dejected, darling. There's one consolation – the loss won't be so great the next time you throw it at me –"

"I won't ever throw it at you again, you know that!" She had hung her head, but it was brought up again as Wayne tilted her chin with his finger.

"You'd better not. Because then," he added significantly, "you'll be my wife – and pay the penalty for such vandalism."

She buried her face in his coat.

"How did you explain it to Avril?" she wanted to know.

"I told her the truth."

"You did!" she ejaculated, going hot and then cold, and at the same time recalling her own conviction that Wayne would endeavour to fob Avril off with some story of his own. "Oh, Wayne, not all of it!"

"I omitted my despicable suggestion, obviously," he replied in a grim tone. "I merely told her we'd quarrelled and that you'd thrown the Sung bowl at me. I also added that I'd deserved it." Kerry said nothing and he continued, "Avril had guessed that I loved you – drawn her own conclusions from my carrying you upstairs, and from my expression when I looked at you – or so she said. There was a – well, a scene, I suppose you would call it, between Avril and me, and she really opened up, making me realize I was all the things you had already called me – No, darling, don't interrupt, because they were all true – at that time. Avril said I was over-protective regarding her money, and she insisted I let her have the money to bring both you and Michelle back to Barbados. It was obvious she didn't know anything about this business you had been hoping she would buy, but I then told her about it. I also said I was coming to England – to ask you to marry me – so of course she wanted to come too."

Wayne ended by telling Kerry that Rowena had left his house, and his employ. "She decided to return to England," he said without much expression, and Kerry was convinced she would never know whether or not there was any truth in the rumours concerning Wayne and his secretary. Nor did she want to know. All that interested her, as she glanced up and saw the depth of love and tenderness in Wayne's eyes, was the sure conviction that there was certainly no truth in Charles's assertion that Wayne could never be true to one woman.

There still remained a little explaining to do, but for the present neither Wayne nor Kerry were willing to waste time on so uninteresting a matter – there being much more enjoyable things to do. But after a long while Kerry broached the subject of Michelle, only to discover that practically everything had been settled, Wayne having instructed Stephen Haslett to deal with the matter of the business for Mrs. Johnson.

"That is," Wayne added a trifle anxiously, "if she still wants it now that she doesn't have her husband to help her."

"She still wants it," Kerry assured him, adding that Mr. Johnson wouldn't have been much help anyway. "Does this mean that we can take Michelle back with us?" Kerry then asked, and Wayne nodded.

"Avril's enchanted with her and it's easy to see that they'll be good company for one another. When Avril is older she will of course move into her own house, and Michelle might want to go with her. For the present, though, they'll remain with us." He looked tenderly at her. "You'll like that, won't you?"

Kerry nodded, swallowing a little lump in her throat.

"Thank you, Wayne," she said simply, and Wayne caught her protectively to him.

"Little did I know I would owe my life's happiness to some unknown woman who was to leave her niece a thousand pounds."

"Neither did I." For a little while Kerry became immersed in reflection. Wayne would never know the misery, the heartache, which that legacy had cost her, for she would never tell him the whole. And suddenly she knew there was nothing to tell, for the misery and heartache were now submerged by the happiness that had come to her, and by the imminent fulfilment of her original desire – the reunion between her two sisters and herself.

"Perhaps," she suggested, shining up at him, "we should be thinking of going to Michelle's. She and Avril will be wondering where we are."

"Perhaps we should," Wayne agreed, but added, suddenly stern, "No tears, mind!"

Kerry supposed he was telling her he'd had quite enough for one day, with Avril and Michelle. There would be many more tears, Kerry surmised, when the time came for Michelle to say goodbye to her mother and the little ones.

"I won't cry," Kerry promised him . . . but she was not quite sure, and so she nestled close, resting her head against his shoulder, as if content to delay the reunion just a little while longer.

Be sure always to look for the name MILLS & BOON on the covers, so that you may be certain the books are genuine MILLS & BOON publications. In case of difficulty in obtaining the books – or if you would like us to send you post free our catalogue – please write to us:

MILLS & BOON LIMITED
17-19 FOLEY STREET
LONDON W1A 1DR